# CROOKED TRUTH

Kristine F. Anderson writes so vividly and confidently of her little postage stamp of Georgia, I couldn't help but imagine Flannery O'Connor and her peacocks watching the goings on in Crisscross with great interest. A true Southern gem.

—Daren Wang, author of *The Hidden Light of Northern Fires*

*Crooked Truth* by Kristine F. Anderson chronicles the journey of a young man from boyhood to manhood. Set in the rural south of the 1940s, the story has the magical ability to transport the reader to another time and place in the world. There is nothing better than a simple story told well, and this book certainly falls into that category. Anderson's skill with the written word captures the angst of life as it once was, yet also leads the reader along the path of hope.

—Raymond L. Atkins, author of *Set List*

Kristine F. Anderson's *Crooked Truth* inhabits the same fictional corner of the universe as *To Kill a Mockingbird* or Ferrol Sams's Porter Osborne trilogy. Her narrator Lucas has a literary lineage that stretches back to Tom Sawyer, and Lucas's uncle Alvin Earl embodies the bigotry and ugliness of every small-town Southern villain from Bob Ewell to Boss Hogg. But Anderson's novel claims its own ground. Her characters are imperfect dreamers, seeking refuge in the past or trying to glimpse a brighter future. Anderson's story touches darkness, but it is not a grim book. Instead, it is hopeful, expansive, and at the same time intimate. Race and class and family secrets are all part of this rich brew. We see through Lucas's eyes the post-WWII South, a world Anderson renders with clarity and detailed historical accuracy without slowing down the story one jot. But Lucas also shows us the world the way young teenagers everywhere see it: full of chores, often dramatic, occasionally tragic, but peopled with dogs and girls and the eternal promise of a chance to go fishing. I was sorry to leave Lucas and his family at the close of this novel, but I am glad that I can revisit them as often as I wish. *Crooked Truth* proudly takes its place in the ranks of Southern literature.

—Christopher Swann, author of *Never Turn Back*

MERCER UNIVERSITY PRESS

*Endowed by*

TOM WATSON BROWN
*and*
THE WATSON-BROWN FOUNDATION, INC.

# Crooked Truth

a novel

## Kristine F. Anderson

MERCER UNIVERSITY PRESS

*Macon, Georgia*

WINNER OF THE
FERROL SAMS AWARD
FOR FICTION

MUP/ P612

ISBN      978-0-88146-757-4
eBook    978-0-88146-758-1

25 24 23 22 21 20      9 8 7 6 5 4 3 2 1

Books published by Mercer University Press are printed on acid-free
paper that meets the requirements of the American National
Standard for Information Sciences—Permanence of Paper for Printed
Library Materials.

Printed and bound in the United States.
This book is set in Adobe Garamond Pro.
Cover/jacket design by Burt&Burt.

Names: Anderson, Kristine F., author.
Title: Crooked truth : a novel / Kristine F. Anderson.
Description: Macon, Georgia : Mercer University Press, [2020] |
Identifiers: LCCN 2020015007 (print) | LCCN 2020015008 (ebook) |
ISBN 9780881467574 (paperback ; acid-free paper)
ISBN 9780881467581 (ebook)

Subjects: fiction
Classification: LCC PS3601.N54428 C76 2020  (print) | LCC PS3601.N54428
    (ebook) | DDC 813/.6--dc23
LC record available at https://lccn.loc.gov/2020015007
LC ebook record available at https://lccn.loc.gov/2020015008

*The truth does not change according to our ability to stomach it.*

—Flannery O'Connor

# Crooked Truth

# SPRING 1948

## 1

Smoke rolled across the yard, almost hiding the old house and shed. I hurled more dead limbs on the fire and caught a whiff of gasoline. "Get back, Robert!" I shouted, tossing some big sticks and chunks of cardboard on the growing pile. "The wind's picking up."

My uncle kept moving toward the blaze as if he hadn't heard me. Slowly circling the burning heap, he threw a handful of dried grass on the flickering flames. He laughed and reached for the bits of ash that floated through the air.

"This trash is going up real fast." I grabbed his arm. "Go over by Granny Lettie." Robert was short, but at least forty pounds heavier than me. Trying to get him to move was like trying to lift a bale of wet cotton.

"I want to watch the fire." His words were thick and he shook me off. "It's real pretty."

"Come sit with me, Robert," called Granny from the back porch. "It's nice and cool up here."

He shuffled toward the porch, his arms hanging by his sides. He slumped down on the cement steps and leaned against the screen door. I threw more branches on the pile.

"Lucas, when you finish burning the limbs, I want you to rake out my rose beds and water them," Granny said. "Robert can help. I'm going in to check on your grandpaw."

I shrugged and frowned. I didn't want to be bothered with watering or with Robert on a beautiful Saturday morning. I'd planned to slip off and go fishing. I'd find a shady spot and smoke a couple of the cigarettes I had hidden in my pocket. And, if I was lucky, hook a catfish.

"Come help me!" I wiped the sweat off my forehead with my sleeve and picked up a rake.

Robert stood up and plodded toward the hose. When he started filling the cans, he got the hose all twisted up, drenching his pants and shoes.

"Watch it. You're sloshing water all over," I said over the steady hum of an approaching truck. "Here comes Alvin Earl. He's driving that new pickup everybody's talking about."

Alvin Earl was forty-six years old and lived in town. He was Robert's older half-brother from Paw Paw's first marriage, making him my step-uncle. Since his mother died long before Paw Paw married my grandmother, he was no blood kin to Granny Lettie, my mother, or me. But even if he were, I wouldn't claim him.

He swung the truck into the drive, churning up gravel and clumps of dirt. Instead of parking in the lot by the barn, he drove between the pecan trees lining the drive. He pulled into the yard real slow, the morning sun bouncing off his grill work. Then he cut off his engine by the back steps, his front wheel almost crushing Granny's azaleas.

"That the new '48 model?" I asked.

"Yeah. It's the only one in the county—maybe the only one in south Georgia." He got out and buffed the door with his sleeve. "You'd likely have to go all the way to Macon to find another one. Look at that finish."

"It's real shiny," said Robert.

"How much did it cost you?" I wondered where he got the money to buy the latest pickup. In all the years I'd been living on the farm, I was never sure what he did. And I knew the latest model cost a heck of a lot more than the used scooter I was saving up to buy in Crisscross.

"A lot more cash than you'll ever have." He kept buffing the door and didn't even glance my way.

"Lucas is rich," shouted Robert, making big circles of water with the hose. "He's got lots of money in his sock."

Alvin Earl's eyes shifted toward me for a split second. "Did he say something about a sock? I can't understand him."

"I don't know what he's talking about." Then I scowled at Robert, putting my finger on my lips. I'd been saving up all the money I got for selling pecans and collecting bottles so I could buy that scooter. I didn't want him telling Alvin Earl or anyone else my business.

"Daddy still in the bed?" Alvin Earl jammed his wrinkled shirt into his pants and smoothed down his hair.

"His shoulder's hurting real bad this morning," I said.

"Did your grandmother call the doctor?"

"No, Paw Paw said he didn't need a doctor." But I knew if Paw Paw wasn't up to working outside today, I'd have extra chores. And I'd be stuck looking after my uncle.

"Doctors don't know a damn thing. They've never done much for him, have they?" Alvin Earl jerked his thumb toward Robert. "What's that boy doin' with that hose? Looks like he's just making a big mess."

Robert was thirteen years older than me, but Alvin Earl usually called him "that boy." Even if Robert were standing next to him, he never called him his brother or used his name.

I hesitated a minute and said, "He's helping me take care of Granny's roses."

"He's twenty-eight years old and playing around in the water like a little kid."

"I want to go for a ride in the truck." Robert moved toward the pickup with his shoelaces trailing in the dirt. When he stumbled on a rock, he dropped the hose like a live wire. Water shot toward the back steps and screened porch.

Alvin Earl jumped all around the yard like he'd just stepped on a hill of ants in his bare feet. I'd never seen him move so fast in my life. He didn't get wet, but the hose sprayed water on the side of his truck. Clamping my lips together, I tried not to laugh and thought that served him right! Maybe next time he'd park in the gravel lot just like everybody else.

I turned off the spigot and Alvin Earl rushed over to inspect his new prize. He cursed Robert in a loud voice and dabbed at the wet spots with his handkerchief. "I'd better not see you crack a smile, Lucas. Look what that boy did."

I forced myself to look serious. Robert mumbled something I couldn't hear and twisted the heel of his shoe in the dirt. Then he ducked behind a magnolia tree in the yard.

"Don't try and hide. Look at me." Alvin Earl's face tightened as he picked up a big stick.

Robert stuck his head out from behind the tree, his eyes lowered to the ground.

"Look at me, boy!" Alvin Earl gripped the stick like a club. "I'd better not see another drop of water on my pickup. Do you understand?"

Robert nodded and ducked behind the tree again.

"He tripped on a rock," I said. "He didn't mean anything."

"I'm watching y'all. There's going to be some changes around here."

"What kind of changes?" I asked, my stomach churning.

"Y'all are going to see a lot more of me now that Daddy's sick. I'm going to be the one running things." Stepping toward me, he jabbed me in the chest with the pointed end of his stick.

I backed away, rubbing the spot where he poked me. It was bad enough when he showed up for free meals. No mat-

4

ter what happened to Paw Paw, I didn't want Alvin Earl hanging around all day telling us what to do. Little George, our hired hand, and I had been taking care of the farm pretty much for the past year. As long as the tractor was running good, we could manage just fine on our own.

"For starters, y'all are going to be spending more time out in the fields. Your grandmother can take care of her own flower garden. Lucas, I want you to wash and wax this truck every week. I want it to look like it just came off the lot."

I'd been driving the tractor since I was eleven and didn't mind working in the fields with Little George. But I wasn't going to take care of his pickup.

"I'll wash your truck if you'll let me drive it—I get my license next year. Or better yet, you can pay me." I knew he'd never let me behind the wheel or give me a dime. But I wanted to hear what he'd say.

"Hell, no. You must be as crazy as that boy if you think I'm going to pay you. And no one's driving this truck but me." Slapping the stick against his thigh, he swaggered toward the kitchen like a four-star general reviewing his troops.

Stop! I wanted to shout. You're not going to push me around. And you're the crazy one if you expect me to clean your pickup and do your chores without any pay. But it seemed like I was always thinking one thing around Alvin Earl and saying something else.

"I need some coffee and biscuits. Get to work and make yourselves useful." Alvin Earl dropped the stick to his side and slammed the porch door behind him.

I coiled up the hose and passed it to Robert. "You heard what he said. I'll turn the water back on." I stooped down and tapped his leg. "Stick out your shoe."

"I can do it, Lucas," said Robert. "I can make loops."

"I know, but I'll tie it with a double knot. Hold still."

5

"Not too tight." He rested his hands on my shoulders for balance.

"You don't want to trip on the laces." I tapped his leg again and stood up. "Now go fill up those cans. And stay away from that truck."

I turned on the water and gathered more brush for the burn pile. Robert started to sprinkle the beds. He worked slowly and steadily—I didn't have to get on him about being careful with the hose. But when he was almost finished, he dropped a can and ducked behind the pump house, his favorite hiding place.

"What are you doing?" I yelled, sweat running down my neck and back.

"I'm hiding. Come find me."

"I told you—we need to get this watering done before Alvin Earl comes back out here. We don't have time for hide-and-seek or any other game." I ground my teeth. The wind had died down and the morning was slipping away. The sun was almost directly overhead. I wanted to find a shady spot by the pond for a cigarette and figure out what to do about Alvin Earl.

"Come find me!"

"No, we've got work to do. But if we ever get to play again, I'll take off on my scooter and be gone for good."

2

I was relieved when Alvin Earl left in his truck that afternoon and didn't hang around for supper. I wanted to drink a Co'Cola and listen to my Saturday night programs without any interruptions. And when I heard the sound of a train whistle coming out of the Philco radio sitting on the kitchen shelf, I knew it was about time for "The Mysterious Traveler."

"What that traveler doin' tonight?" Corinthia asked, drying her hands on a kitchen towel. She was in a hurry to go home with Little George.

"He's going to the pyramids to search for grave robbers and an ancient mummy," I said, sipping my cold drink and wishing I could hop on a boxcar and head someplace famous instead of being stuck in a little town in South Georgia.

"For a mummy?" asked Robert, picking at a mole on his elbow with his thumbnail.

"You don't even know what a mummy is." I was still pissed because I'd had to watch him earlier in the day and hadn't gotten to go fishing. "And quit messing with that mole—it's going to start to bleed."

"Robert, you take your Co'Cola and go on in with your momma and daddy," said Corinthia. "You don't need to be listenin' to no stuff 'bout dead people walkin' 'round in somebody's ol' sheets."

Robert jerked his chin out and shook his head. "I want to stay with Lucas."

"Go on," I said. "You'll wake me up in the middle of the night screaming if you stay in here. We can listen to the ball games another night."

"Hurry up, now," said Corinthia. "Little George out in the shed waitin' for me. After workin' all day, he be wantin' his supper."

"You promise?" Robert asked me, scraping his chair on the wooden floor as he picked up his Co'Cola.

"Yeah, I promise. Now go on in with Granny."

"I'm going to play 'Oh, My Darling Clementine'—one of your favorites, Robert," Granny called. "Lucas, come in and sing with your uncle."

Granny used to teach piano when my mother was young. She had an old metronome that Robert loved to hear and stacks of music stuffed in the bookcase. But she only played folk tunes and music from the great composers—she never played any big band melodies. And sometimes when the church ladies were here and she was all dressed up, she played hymns like "What a Friend We Have in Jesus" and "The Old Rugged Cross."

"It's almost time for my program," I grumbled, thinking I was the only high school kid in the world who had to sing about a miner's daughter on a Saturday night.

"This won't take long." Granny plunked out the melody. "You know how Paw Paw likes to hear y'all sing."

I went into the parlor and half-heartedly joined in. While Paw Paw dozed in his favorite chair with *The Crisscross Crier* on his lap, I studied the pictures that filled the room. Except for the color portrait of President Roosevelt hanging above the fireplace, all of the pictures were black and white photos of the family and my classes in elementary school.

My eyes rested on a framed snapshot of my mother and Robert taken right before my parents were killed in the car wreck. She's smiling and reading him a picture book on the back porch. She was almost twelve years older than Robert and had a different father, but they both had wispy blond hair, turquoise green eyes, and dimples. And even though I was tall and lanky and, for some reason, only had one dimple and crooked front teeth, most folks said I favored my mother, too.

As we sang, I heard Alvin Earl come in the back door and poke around the kitchen, searching for some leftover supper. When he couldn't find anything to eat, he came into the parlor and leaned against the wall. He wore a starched white shirt, and his shoes had more polish on them than

Granny's piano. He'd slicked back his hair to hide his bald spot, and I could smell the Vitalis from across the room. A little dab of toilet paper clung to his chin, soaking up the blood from a shaving nick. And he had a cigarette stuck behind his ear.

Granny droned on, and I heard a deep voice announcing tonight's episode. Fixing my eyes on the mantel clock, I slowly inched towards the kitchen, eager to make my escape.

Robert, enjoying an audience, started another round of "Clementine" and swayed to the music. He had a high, sweet voice, but little bubbles of spit popped up on his lip when he sang. And he always got the words mixed up.

After he finished the last line, Alvin Earl clapped and asked, "You can train a monkey or dog to do tricks. Which one is he?"

Granny jerked her pale fingers off the keys and froze. Alvin Earl's question hung in the air like a bad note and silence filled the room. When no one answered, he asked again, "Is he a trained monkey or a circus dog doing tricks?"

Glancing at Robert, I knew he didn't catch the sarcasm in Alvin Earl's voice or understand his question. He thought it was funny and laughed. "I'm not a monkey. I'm not a dog. I'm your brother."

"I don't get a word he's saying. He talks like he's got a mouthful of grits." Pulling out his lighter with the one-eyed Jack insignia, he flipped the top open. Then he spun the little rubber wheel around with his thumb.

Robert stared at the silver lighter and Granny frowned. "If you'd spend some time with Robert, you wouldn't have any problem understanding him. We never have any problems understanding him, do we, Harold?"

Paw Paw, looking old and tired, stirred in his chair and opened his eyes. He scowled at Alvin Earl. "None at all."

Then Granny turned toward Robert and smiled. "Alvin Earl knows you're his brother. He's just joking with you."

"Yeah, you want to go for a ride in my new truck, boy?" Alvin Earl said with a sneer. "We could go into Crisscross and play some cards. I'm feeling real lucky tonight."

Robert reached into his pocket and held up a shiny penny Little George had given him a couple of years ago. "I got a lucky piece."

"That's enough!" Paw Paw threw down his newspaper. "Let's hear you boys sing again."

"Go on, boys," said Alvin Earl in a hard voice. "Maybe y'all will get on the radio. Lucas, you could put Robert on your lap and pretend he's one of those dummies with a top hat. He'd be a natural."

Granny caught Paw Paw's eye and her hands dropped into her lap. There was another heavy silence. The only thing I could hear was the faint voice of the announcer and the organ music coming from the kitchen.

Paw Paw stood up. Wagging his finger in Alvin Earl's face, he said, "That's enough. We don't need any more talk about dummies, and if you need to smoke, go out on the porch!"

Alvin Earl was four or five inches taller than Paw Paw and at least fifty pounds heavier, but he took a quick step back. "You know I didn't mean anything, Daddy. I was just playing with him."

"Find another game," Paw Paw ordered, gripping the back of a chair for support.

"Anything you say, Daddy. I was just having a little fun." Alvin Earl slipped his lighter back in his pocket and headed through the kitchen to the back door.

"Where's he going?" asked Robert.

"None of your business," Paw Paw said in a gruff voice as he followed Alvin Earl to the kitchen.

"You don't want to know," I whispered to Robert.

Granny hurried over to Paw Paw and laid her hand on his arm, trying to hold him back. "He's getting in his truck and he's going back into town," she said in a soothing voice.

"I paid all that money to dry him out in that fancy hospital in Atlanta, and now he's probably going to Gordy's Garage to drink and play cards with his old crowd," Paw Paw said under his breath.

"He didn't drink when he first came back home and slept in his room," Granny said.

"How long did that last?" muttered Paw Paw. "Not even a week."

I'd heard folks talking about Alvin Earl hanging around Gordy's, but I never heard anything about him going to a hospital in Atlanta. When he'd disappeared for a month, Paw Paw and Granny said he'd gone to visit some old friends.

"Is he coming back?" asked Robert.

"I don't know and I don't care." I went in the kitchen to hear the mysterious traveler entering the tomb. "I don't want him hanging around here and neither do Granny and Paw Paw."

## 3

A few days later I was studying a newspaper ad for a Cushman scooter when Robert plopped down next to me on the front porch swing. The sun was easing over the pecan trees along the drive and there was a slight breeze.

"What are you doing?" he asked over the creak of the old swing.

"Leave me alone. I'm reading about scooters."

Not to be put off, Robert reached in his pocket and pulled out the bit of string he always carried. Wrapping it around his head, he let out a loud war cry and tugged on my arm. "Chase me, Lucas!"

"No! Go out in the yard if you want to run around."

"You come, too," he pleaded.

"Are you deaf? I'm reading."

"I want to read, too." Robert leaned over and squinted at the small print.

"You care about scooters about as much as you do about baseball. Go play with Granny's metronome or get your cap gun." I could never shake Robert loose when I was on the farm. He was worse than a piece of roofing tar stuck on the sole of my shoe. The more I tried to pull away from him, the more he wanted to stay with me. I couldn't even take a piss without him hanging over my shoulder.

"I don't have any caps," he whined. Letting out another war hoop, he grabbed my hand and tried to pull me up. "Let's go count the money."

"What money?"

"The money in your drawer." He pointed to our bedroom.

"Shhh! I don't want everyone to know where I keep it. Now let go. You're crushing my fingers."

I stood up and walked toward our bedroom, Robert following right behind. "Make sure you close the door tight," I said.

After I checked the door, I opened up a small desk drawer. I carefully took out the old sock where I'd hidden my money, and we sat down on the floor Indian style. But Robert's overalls were so tight he could barely cross his legs. His socks were inside out and his shoe was untied. As usual, he didn't have his glasses on.

"Robert, where's your glasses?"

He pointed to the table between our beds. He'd sat on his glasses one morning and bent the frames. As if he didn't look strange enough already, Granny had wrapped thick adhesive tape around the nose bridge for extra support.

While he fitted the temple piece over each ear, I dumped all the change and bills onto the rag rug. With the two dollars I'd gotten for my last birthday, I knew I had exactly $7.12, almost the amount I needed to buy the used scooter.

Rubbing his hands together, Robert looked at me over his glasses. "Okay, Lucas. I'm ready."

"Let's put the coins in piles—a brown pile and a pile for the big silver ones and another pile for the little silver ones." He didn't understand the value of the coins, but he loved to play with anything smooth and shiny. Handling the money was like a game to him.

After I counted out the bills, I said, "Remember the quarters have the picture of George Washington."

"He was real important." Robert concentrated on putting the coins in different piles. He pointed to each coin with his finger. "You're rich. Can we go to the Hopalong Cassidy movie?"

"No. I'm saving up for a scooter with a kick starter."

"Can I ride it?"

Robert used to hold on to my seat when I was learning how to ride a two-wheeler. But he never learned to ride a bike himself, and I knew he'd never be able to ride the scooter. Nodding, I kept counting and said, "Sure."

As we totaled up the piles, someone pushed the door open and I heard a familiar clicking sound. Alvin Earl slouched against the doorway, flipping his silver lighter open and closed. Robert stared at the lighter and reached out for it.

"You like my lighter, boy?" he asked, rolling his thumb across the tiny wheel until a flame appeared. He stooped down and flashed the flame in front of Robert's face. "Ain't that pretty?"

"Yeah." Robert held out his hand. "I want to do it."

"I bet you do." Alvin Earl held up his lighter to catch the sunlight pouring in our window, his fingers tightening on the Jack's face. "I won this off some guy from the Klan."

"The Ku Klux Klan?" I asked. "My history teacher said they died out."

"Ha! Your teacher ain't up-to-date. They're still around Atlanta. Ask Little George and some of the other niggers around here." Sticking the lighter back in his pocket, he pulled out a deck of cards. "Where'd you get all the money?"

"From working in Granny's garden and cleaning up the cemetery." I gathered the piles and stuck everything in my pocket. I didn't want him looking at my savings.

"I thought you boys had been doing some gambling in Crisscross." He waited for me to laugh while he shuffled his deck, but I didn't think his joke was funny. Fanning the cards out on our dresser top in one smooth motion, he winked at me. "What are you going to do with all that cash?"

"Buy a scooter," Robert said.

"A scooter? Is that what he said?" Alvin Earl asked, looking at me as I were some kind of a translator. "What do you need a scooter for? There's an old bike in the barn."

"I know, but the tires are bad." I stood up and so did Robert.

"That used to be my bike. My mother paid good money for it."

"That bike's at least thirty years old and the tires are rotted out. You can't expect me to ride that."

"There's a heck of a lot of things we need around here a lot more than a scooter. And I wouldn't let Four-eyes touch my money." Waving his hand at Robert, he let out a mean chuckle.

"Four-eyes?" Robert asked. "I've only got two eyes. See?" He lifted up his glasses with one hand and held up two fingers on his other hand.

"He can count to two, but I bet he can't recognize the numbers on the cards." Alvin Earl picked up the eight of hearts and flashed it in Robert's face. "How many?"

Robert peered at the card and took a step closer to get a better look. Then he started tugging on his ear, something he did whenever he got nervous or scared.

"You know what a heart is?" Alvin Earl thumped his chest. "How many are on the card?"

Robert looked at me, hoping I'd give him a hint. But I stared out the window, studying the old "Piano Lessons" sign Granny had posted by the mailbox when she and Paw Paw first got married.

"Come on, come on. I haven't got all day, boy."

Robert blinked and looked at me again, but I turned away. He moved closer to count the hearts on the card. Using his finger, he said, "One, two, three, five, seven. Seven!"

"Seven!" Alvin Earl said with disgust. "There's eight! He can't even count the hearts on a card."

Robert mumbled something and started counting again. I pushed a pencil back and forth across my desk with my thumb, avoiding looking at Alvin Earl or Robert.

Planting his feet wide, Alvin Earl stuck the card back in the deck. "He's like a three-year-old in a man's body. Everybody knows that except his momma." He stomped out, bumping into Corinthia in his rush.

"Oh, 'cuse me, Mr. Alvin Earl," Corinthia said as she opened the door and squeezed into our bedroom with a stack of clean shirts.

He glared at her. Then he stormed through the kitchen to the porch, slamming the screen door behind him.

"Where he goin' in such a hurry?" Corinthia demanded.

"I don't know," I said, hoping the door hit him in the ass. "He just left."

"He was real mad," Robert said.

"I knows he mad, but that man forty-six years old. He don't need to be makin' all that racket when Mr. Harold restin'."

"He's probably got a card game going at Gordy's," I said.

"His daddy won't like that, but ain't much he can do 'bout it."

Alvin Earl lived in a small house in Crisscross. When I was in elementary school, he was married to a pretty young girl with dimples named Betty Jean. She looked a little like my mother and loved to laugh. One year, she gave me a Parcheesi game for Christmas. But a few months later, she moved out.

After Betty Jean left him, Granny said, "We probably won't be seeing much of that poor girl now." She stuck their wedding picture in a kitchen drawer and put up a picture of me winning the high school regional essay contest in its place. Sometimes, when no one was around, I looked at the picture in the drawer and wondered if Betty Jean still had her dimples.

Some folks said she divorced Alvin Earl because he drank and did things nice folks didn't discuss. When I asked my grandmother what kind of things Alvin Earl did when he was married, she simply said, "Betty Jean was as sweet as she could be, but I'm thankful there weren't any children." Then she added, "Just remember, Lucas, one day we'll all stand before God, and He'll separate the sheep from the goats."

"Where's Betty Jean now?"

"I'm not sure. She might be living with her mother. Go ask Paw Paw."

I went out on the porch and asked Paw Paw what happened to Betty Jean. He looked at me for a few seconds and then shifted his glance to the front fields. "Alvin Earl was too young to get married and take on a wife." Brushing by me, he walked out to the shed, leaving me standing alone on the porch.

4

"Move, Robert, you're in my way," I said.

"I'm making rabbit ears."

"You're sitting right in front of the dresser. I'm trying to get dressed and I'm hungry."

He didn't budge. Dressed in a plaid shirt and his underwear, he hunched over his shoes, wrapping his laces around his fingers.

"Your loops are way too big."

"I can make the ears. I can do it."

"I know you can, but you need to put your overalls on before you tie your shoes. How many times do I have to tell you?"

When I bent down to help him make a smaller loop, he rolled over onto one cheek and let out a huge fart. "That's terrible, Robert—that smells worse than a dead chicken that's been stuck up your butt."

"Excuse me," he said with a giggle. And then he farted again.

Rushing out of the bedroom, I said, "You can tie your own shoes. I can't stand it in here."

I shut the bedroom door and headed to the kitchen for breakfast. The smell of fresh coffee and sausage covered the smell of Robert's farts. Corinthia already had the biscuits on the table and was pouring red-eye gravy into a bowl.

"Mornin', Lucas," she said. "Ready for your breakfast?"

I frowned and sat down.

"You can't say good mornin'?"

"I want my own bedroom and some privacy."

"What you talkin' 'bout?" asked Corinthia in a sharp voice. "That Robert's room long 'fore you come along. He made a place for you. And when you first come here, he tote you all 'round this farm like you his special baby. If he weren't totin' you, he pullin' you in his little red cart. He took carea you 'til you ol' 'nough to go to school."

I shook my head. "I ain't a little kid anymore. I can't even go to the bathroom without Robert hanging over my shoulder."

"You can discuss that with Mr. Harold. But you best remember you might not be standin' here if Robert hadn't been 'round to sling that copperhead out in the woods when it come after you. You barely four years old then—a snake bite coulda killed you."

I'd heard this story before, but my mind flashed back to that day at the woodpile more than ten years ago. I didn't see the snake, but Robert did. He shouted "Stand still" and grabbed a long stick. Crying because he yelled at me, I watched him pick up the brown and black snake and toss it into the backwoods. Then I waited for him to pick me up and tell me everything was all right.

I was still afraid of snakes. But I didn't want to let on to Corinthia that I remembered the day. Instead, I reached for the sorghum syrup.

Corinthia yanked me up by the collar. She dragged me out to the back porch, her knuckles digging into the back of my neck. "A lot of folks sleepin' with three and four in a bed and usin' a pot in the corner. And some folks sleepin' in shacks with a dirt floor. I gets real tired hearin' you fussin' 'bout your uncle all the time. You ol' 'nough to think 'bout him some."

I smoothed down my collar and shrugged. "Everyone's always thinking about Robert."

Corinthia straightened up and put her hands on her hips. "You knows why? Robert a changa-life baby. He born when Miz Lettie almost forty-seven years ol'. And she already buried one chil' 'fore he come along."

"I know, I know." I let out a long sigh, staring at the bowl of biscuits back in the kitchen.

"Well, maybe you needs remindin'. Cuz nothin' tear at your heart like loosin' a chil'." Her eyes shifted and she looked out at the yard, fixing her eyes on something I couldn't see.

I figured she was thinking about Nathan T., her son. After the Japs bombed Pearl Harbor, he wanted to join the army. Corinthia told him he had no business fighting in a white man's war, but the day he turned eighteen, he hitched a ride to Atlanta and enlisted. If he were still alive, he'd be a few years younger than Robert. But he was reported missing in action somewhere in Italy midway through the war. They'd never received his body or remains, and Corinthia and Little George still prayed for his safe return.

As I moved toward the kitchen, she hung on my arm. "You knows the doctor tell Miz Lettie Robert gonna have heart problems and ain't never gonna develop right. He say she need to send him to the state hospital in Maysville. But Miz Lettie die 'fore she send him off. So we cares for him at home cuz no one 'spect him to live long."

"And they were afraid to give him a name. He couldn't nurse. You had to feed him with a bottle. And he didn't sit up or crawl." I could recite this story practically word for word, and I was ready for my breakfast.

"He real colicky and always frettin'. But they went ahead and name him Robert Spencer for Miz Lettie's daddy—he a preacher somewhere near Macon. As soon as they name him, he got fat and healthy. And pretty soon, he start movin' 'round just like the other kids. That Robert fool us all."

"He eats like a horse. He eats more than Alvin Earl."

"Nothin' wrong with his appetite."

"But he's not normal." I lowered my voice so Granny and Robert couldn't hear. "He's a Mongoloid and he's never going to be normal. Everyone knows that, except Granny."

"Oh, deep down she know—most womens knows the truth 'bout their kids. She just don't wanna talk 'bout it." Wiping off the porch table with the corner of her apron, she leaned toward me and added, "Just cuz he couldn't go to school with the other kids in town don't mean he stupid. He can do a lot more than my nephew Caleb. Caleb sets in a chair all day and kinda grunts. If his momma don't watch him like a hawk, he mess his pants."

"Why doesn't she send him to the asylum in Maysville?" My stomach rumbled, begging for food.

"Oh, she never do that! There way too many folks at that place and it real nasty. The commodes always gettin' clogged up and it smell bad. And they got roaches big as a bus runnin' 'round the kitchen."

Granny and Paw Paw never talked about the state hospital, but I'd heard lots of stories about the loony bin at school. And sometimes I'd hear parents threaten to send their kids to Maysville if they didn't behave. Telling a kid they were going to Maysville was worse than telling them they were getting a whipping and then making them go outside to get a switch.

"Have you been there?" I asked.

She nodded and kept wiping the table with her apron. "My auntie work in the kitchen when Little George and me first marry. She stay on the grounds and we use' to go visit her."

"Is she still working there?"

"No, she gone. But she say if folks ain't crazy when they first checks in, they goes crazy real quick. And the coloreds even worse off. Mosta 'em locked up in the insane unit for criminals."

"I thought it was supposed to be a hospital."

She shook her head. "They gots way too many folks there and not 'nough doctors and nurses. Sometimes they puts the real crazy-like folks in tubsa cold water or sticks 'em in cages. And some folks just be runnin' 'round naked."

"Does Granny know some patients are in cages and others are running around naked?"

"I ain't told her, Lucas, and I don't think you should neither. I just tellin' you what my auntie done told us."

"So what's going to happen to Caleb when your sister's not around?"

"I don't know what gonna happen when she pass." She picked up the fly swatter hanging next to the porch door. "I can't take carea him if I workin' all day and I gots to work."

"What's going to happen to Robert?"

"I don't know, Lucas. When your momma alive, she real good to him and you needs to be good to him, too." She flecked my shoulder with her fly swatter to make sure I was paying attention.

I thought about the snapshot of my mother reading to Robert on the back porch. "Did she spend a lot of time with Robert?"

"Oh, she call him Bobby and play with him whenever she 'round. She like to read that Winnie-the-Pooh book to him. He loved hearin' 'bout how that bear always lookin' for the honey."

I knew all about that fat little bear and had fuzzy memories of my mother reading Winnie-the-Pooh to me, too. Over the years, I'd read the book to him at least a million times. And even though the stuffed Pooh Bear my mother had given him was real nasty and missing its red sweater, he still slept with it every night.

"He wanna hear that story every time she come to the house," Corinthia continued. "But after she and your daddy got hit by that big truck..." Her voiced trailed off and she didn't finish.

I winced when she mentioned the accident that killed my parents when I was three. But I locked my arms across my chest and stared straight ahead. "I bet she never had to share a room with him or help him shave."

5

The next morning I heard Sam barking as soon as I went into the kitchen. It was barely 6:30, but I knew Little George, our longtime hired hand, was in the yard. I could hear him whistling "Swing Low, Sweet Chariot," one of his favorite tunes, in between the barking. During planting and harvest season, he came to work extra early and Sam always announced his arrival. Some days Sam acted more like a four-legged rooster with a collar than a champion bird dog.

"Good morning, Little George," called Granny through the screen door. "Sam's been waiting for you. Mr. Harold may own him, but he's your dog."

"Lotsa dogs gets real attached to their trainers, Miz Lettie. I gonna feed him in a few minutes, but I ain't gonna have much time to work him today. We gots too much to do."

"Mr. Harold says he'll be out a little bit later this morning," Granny said. "His shoulder's bothering him. Is Cotton working today?"

"He better show up. He s'pose to fix that tractor and help me with them fences."

"I need to check on Mr. Harold," said Granny. "Let's hope Cotton can get the tractor running today."

"He will—he like messin' 'round with engines almost as much as he like playin' ball," said Little George when I walked out on the porch.

Cotton, better known as "The Flame Thrower," had been helping out on the farm since he was about eight or nine. Since his daddy was white, Cotton had straw-colored hair and green eyes. He was Little George's nephew, but he was even lighter than his uncle. He was a few years older than me and had lived with Little George and Corinthia most of his life. A lefty, he'd been the star pitcher at the colored high school in Crisscross before he graduated. And folks said he could throw a ball close to ninety miles an hour.

"I hear Cotton got himself a truck," I said. "You lend him the money?"

"No, I ain't gonna lend him money just cuz he my sister's boy. He been savin' up and bought that ol' Ford pickup at Gordy's. Here he come now." Little George took a couple of steps toward the house, tilting to the side as he walked, and pointed toward the driveway.

Tooting his horn, Cotton pulled into the yard waving his high school baseball cap like a grand marshal parading through Crisscross on the Fourth of July. But splotches of rust covered the truck's hood and door instead of red, white, and blue bunting. The windshield was cracked, and the brakes squealed when he stopped in the yard. He fiddled with the creaky door handle and eased himself out of his truck as if he had all the time in the world.

"Mornin'. Y'all like my truck?"

"That's one sorry vehicle," I said. "Gordy probably couldn't wait to get it off his back lot. But at least you got yourself some transportation." At the rate I was going, I figured it would take me almost a year before I had enough money to buy the Cushman scooter.

"It ain't ever been wrecked." Cotton ran his hand along one of the few smooth spots on the hood. "I gonna get some parts and fix it up real nice. And maybe, if you lucky, I lets you drive it."

"You think that truck can make it to town and back to the farm?" I looked at the tires and shook my head. "It sounds worse than Granny's old wringer washer."

"It gotta have a lot more than new brakes and a muffler, for sure," Little George said. "But get on out to the barn now, Cotton, and see why that tractor so slow to crank."

"I goin'," Cotton said. "See you later, Lucas." Brushing past me, he slipped me the cigarette he had stuck beyond his ear and punched my arm.

"You and Robert goin' fishin' today, Lucas?" asked Little George.

"As soon as I finish my chores." I sighed, hoping I could slip off for once without my uncle.

Robert would rather spend time watching the turtles or looking for sparkly stones at the pond than fish. He cried when he had to stick a hook into a worm, but he liked to walk in the woods with me. And after my friend J.T. moved back to Albany, Granny usually made me take Robert along.

"You know your momma always felt bad for the worms," said Little George.

"That sounds just like Robert," I said, thinking they were more alike in some ways than I'd realized.

"Yep. Where he be this mornin'?"

"He's gathering eggs, but here he comes now."

"Look, everyone." Robert walked toward the house carrying a basket with both hands. "Look what I got."

Little George whistled in approval. "You must be treatin' your hens real nice. I believe they the best layers in Crisscross."

Robert grinned and set the basket on the porch steps while I rolled my eyes. He collected the eggs, but I had to go out to the dusty coop to check the hens and give them fresh feed and water early every morning. And I had to pick up any dead hens before Granny would let him go into the coop.

"Where that Houdini hen?" asked Little George.

"I already put her back," I said. One of the bigger hens refused to lay in the boxes. I started calling her Houdini when she managed to fly over the fence even after we added extra wire to make it taller. She'd lay her egg right next to the back steps as if she wanted to offer us a special gift. After I picked up her egg, I'd stick her back in the fence, knowing she'd fly out again the next morning.

Even though I kind of liked Houdini's independent nature, I never liked going into the smelly old coop. But Robert didn't seem to mind. He didn't notice all the flies or the chicken crap mixed in with the dirt on the floor. Every morning, he greeted the hens in a quiet, soothing voice, and some-times he even sang to them. He treated them like his pets, giving them all names like Flossie and Sugar Pie.

When Corinthia wanted to fry up a hen, she had to wring its neck when Robert was out of sight. Granny didn't want to take a chance on him seeing a bird running around the yard with its head cut off. If he asked what happened to one of his pets, Corinthia simply said a coon or possum must have snuck into the coop while everyone was asleep. Then she'd add, "Mr. Harold need to get his shotgun and go after them critters."

But one morning before I could get into the coop, Robert found Clementine, one of his favorite hens, dead. He brought her body back into the bedroom. I walked in and saw the chicken stretched out on his bed next to his Pooh Bear. She looked even worse than his dirty old bear. "Jesus, Robert! What are you doing?"

"Clementine needs a nice place to sleep." He huddled over the limp hen and stroked her head.

"That chicken's dead. Look at it! And you've got chicken shit all over the floor."

"She's sleeping. Don't wake her up."

"She's dead and she's going to start to smell. You've got to get her out of here." As I moved closer to the bed to look at the hen, Robert pushed me into the dresser, almost knock-ing the small mirror onto the floor.

"Hey, that hurt." I massaged my arm and flexed it up and down. "What did you do that for?"

"You get away and stay away! She's my chickie."

"I know she's your chickie. But you better not let Corin-thia or Granny see her on your bed."

"She's sleeping." His voice broke and he blinked away his tears.

"Robert, sometimes the smaller hens die when the coop gets real hot and crowded. You know that."

"She was just too little." His chest heaving, he stroked the bird's feathers.

I nodded. "Don't you want her to go to heaven with the angels so she can be with the other chickens from the farm? Let's wrap her in some nice soft material from Granny's piece box and take her outside."

Turning his back to me, he shook his head.

"Come on," I coaxed. "We'll find a spot for Clementine and then we can play hide-and-seek."

Robert shook his head again, and I knew I'd have to up the ante. "Maybe we can go into town and see the new Hopalong Cassidy movie. You always like to see Hoppy jump on Topper and go after the bad guys."

"I don't want to see a movie. I want to take care of Clementine."

"Okay, okay. I'll leave you alone." I went into Granny's sewing room and pulled a torn tee-shirt out of her piece box.

I went back into the bedroom and handed Robert the old shirt. "You can wrap her up real nice and we'll bury her."

After he wiped the snot from his nose, he scooped up his bird and wound the soft cotton around her. When he made sure she was completely covered, he sat on the side of his bed, holding her like a tiny baby. Then he rocked her back and forth as he hummed "Jesus Loves Me."

Knowing Granny would have a fit if she ever found out we buried a dead chicken in the family cemetery, I said, "We'll find a place near the roses. The ground's real soft back there. We can dig a hole deep enough to keep the coyotes away."

"She'll grow back?" He looked at me hopefully, his glasses wet from tears.

"No, no. She's not coming back. Burying your chicken's not like planting a seed." Throwing my arm around his shoulders, I tried to explain. "Clementine's going to heaven with the angels. And someday, you'll see her when you go to heaven. But now you can say a prayer and plant something on the grave just like we did with my mother and daddy."

"Plant something?" He wiped his eyes.

"Yeah, you know how we plant flowers on the graves in the family cemetery? You can plant a flower to remember how special Clementine was." Pausing a minute, I added, "I'll help you."

6

A few days later, Robert and I went fishing but didn't catch much big enough to keep. We came back from the pond, sweaty and sunburned with an empty bucket. As soon as we stepped onto the back porch, Corinthia called, "Don't let them flies in. Supper's almost ready."

Robert headed to the bathroom. I stuck our poles in the corner and hung up my cap. I could smell pork chops frying and knew there'd be biscuits in the oven. Walking into the kitchen, I said, "We didn't have much luck today—seems like all the fish disappeared when J.T. moved."

"Mr. Alvin Earl comin' by, so I figured I'd best fix somethin'," she said. "You know how much he eat."

"He doesn't care what you're cooking. He just wants a free meal."

"Who knows what that man want? When he call up here this mornin', he say he need to talk to his daddy 'bout somethin' real important. He pullin' in the drive now."

"He's probably going to ask Paw Paw for money to make the payment on his truck."

Nodding, Corinthia grabbed her fly swatter as Alvin Earl flung open flung the screen door. "Don't you be bringin' in any flies and trackin' mud in on my clean floors. You wipe those nasty lookin' boots on the mat."

"You frying up one of Robert's hens?" He sniffed around the kitchen like an old hound looking for his bone.

"We don't talk 'bout fryin' Robert's hens. I got some pork chops," she said.

"Give me some tea, Corinthia," he demanded, dragging his feet across the mat.

"Tea already out." She pointed to the table with her swatter. "Just go in and set down. Supper ready."

"Come on boys, we're waiting for the blessing," Granny called from the other room.

"Hurry up now," Paw Paw said. "Y'all know I don't like eating cold food."

After we sat down, Robert bowed his head and then looked up to see if I'd bowed mine.

"Go on. Say the blessing," ordered Alvin Earl. "I'm starving."

Robert recited the simple grace everyone learned in the first grade Sunday school class—*God is great, God is good. Let us thank Him.* But that was about all anyone said during supper. Despite all of Granny's efforts to make conversation, eating was serious business. We concentrated on filling our plates. We passed bowls of okra and beans while Corinthia stood by the door with her swatter, ready to chase any insect with wings out of the dining room.

Watching my step-uncle at the table made me sick. Tonight, Alvin Earl ate even faster than usual because he wanted to speak with Paw Paw. He chewed with his mouth open and slurped his tea, wiping his mouth on his shirtsleeve or on the edge of the tablecloth just to irritate Granny. He grabbed second helpings and surrounded himself with the vegetable bowls as if they were his personal property. And he scratched his head with his fork like someone with a bad case of lice.

"You've got a clean napkin next to your plate, Alvin Earl," Granny hinted. But he ignored her, pushing his chair back when he finished and belching loud enough to make the glasses shake.

"Daddy, I'm going out to have a smoke on the front porch."

"I'll be out after I finish my supper." Paw Paw checked his pocket watch and took another helping of okra.

"I'll be waiting." Scrubbing his teeth with his tongue, Alvin Earl pulled out his lighter and flipped it open and closed.

"Excuse me, Granny." I got up from the table and quickly pushed in my chair. "I've got a lot of homework."

When I headed toward my bedroom, Corinthia hissed, "Curiosity kill the cat."

"I ain't no cat." I went into my room so I could listen to Alvin Earl through the screened window. As soon as Paw Paw went out on the porch, Alvin Earl started up.

"I know you're slowing down some, Daddy, but it ain't right letting that gimpy nigger and Corinthia manage things. She's always running her mouth and that yellow nigger's spookin' around all the time."

I heard the creak of the old swing as Paw Paw sat down and chuckled. "Everyone in Crisscross knows Corinthia runs the kitchen. But she ain't running the farm."

"She would if she could and you know it. They should head North with all the other niggers."

"Little George's family has been in Crisscross almost as long as we have. Even with his bad leg, he can do the work of three men. And Cotton's a good worker, too."

"That still don't make it right. Little George drives your truck around town and buys seed and fertilizer like he owns the place. He thinks he's so damn smart—one of these days, he'll find out he's too smart for his own good."

"What are you talking about? He's been hanging around here since he was a little kid," said Paw Paw. "Your momma just didn't want you playing with him or any other colored kids. She was scared to death you'd get worms or some other disease if you got too close to them. That's why she took you off the farm and moved back into town, in case you don't remember."

"Well, some folks are starting to talk."

"Who? And since when did you start caring what folks say?"

"This farm is going be mine one day," Alvin Earl countered. "I'll come back and help out."

"You've got your own life now. Little George knows every inch of this property and he's good with the animals. He's the best trainer in south Georgia."

"Maybe, but how much longer are you gonna be hunting? Sam's getting pretty old."

"Who knows? My name ain't been listed in the obituaries yet and neither has Sam's. Lots of folks are still offering me stud fees for his services."

"What about the field work? You can't afford to buy one of those new mechanical pickers."

"Ha, I could use a new tractor, but I wouldn't spend my money on one of them machines even if I could. From what I hear, they're always breaking down and you got to get new parts. Between the two of them, Little George and Cotton can pick over five hundred pounds of cotton a day. They could go down a row with their eyes closed. By the time they finish, there ain't enough left to make a pillow."

"What about Lucas?"

"He can pick close to two hundred pounds a day. And Little George will hire some pickers to come in."

"Lucas could do a lot more in the fields if you pulled him out of school and he worked year-round."

"I want to pull him out, but Miss Lettie won't hear of it. She wants him to get a scholarship and go on to college."

I leaned closer to the screened window, eager to hear more. Even though I wasn't sure what I was going to do when I finished high school, I knew I wanted to travel some. I sure didn't see myself hanging around Crisscross working for Alvin Earl on the farm.

"What about Robert? He's strong, but you've got to watch him every minute."

"Miss Lettie doesn't want him out in the fields. She's afraid he'll strain his heart. Corinthia keeps her eyes on him."

"She'd better. A chicken's got more sense than that boy. He needs to be in the state hospital."

"His mother would never let him go to Maysville. Besides, he's still your half-brother and carries the family name."

"That may be, but I'm your oldest son. I'm the one who inherits the farm and your gun collection."

I took a quick peek through the window. I saw Alvin Earl stroll toward his truck and then turn to get the last word. "And managing the farm is between you and me."

7

Bright red and pink flowers covered Granny's azaleas and the dogwoods were blooming. It was getting closer to planting time. Little George and Cotton were spending more hours working in the fields. The days were getting longer. And we only had two more months of school.

When I walked into the kitchen for some breakfast on Saturday morning, Corinthia had the counter fan going full blast. But it already felt hot and sticky.

"Mornin', Lucas," she said, putting the gravy on the table. "Where Robert?"

"He's still getting dressed." I sat down and reached for the eggs. "You got any more biscuits?"

"Where your manners? How 'bout a please?" She put more biscuits on the table and fanned herself with her apron. "That stove just make it hotter. I tol' Little George he gotta get out in the fields early today."

"What about Cotton?" I grabbed a couple of biscuits and covered them with gravy.

"He out in the shed workin' on that ol' tractor. Slow down, now. You eatin' breakfast, not goin' to the horse races."

"I want to get those beds watered." I ate quickly, then dragged the back of my hand across my mouth as I pushed my chair back and headed to the yard. I couldn't wait to get out of the kitchen and away from Corinthia's sharp eyes.

"Hey, Lucas," called Cotton from the shed. "Gonna be another hot one. What y'all doin' today?"

"I've got to work in Granny's garden and the cemetery. And then I'm going fishing. You want to come along?"

"You the fishin'est man 'round, but you ain't had much luck since your buddy moved back to Albany."

"Somehow J.T. knew where to find the biggest cats in the pond. He was born to fish." I kicked the gravel and laughed when I thought of all the fish J.T. reeled in.

"Y'all did a lot more than wet a line, and I knows it wasn't schoolwork." Cotton propped his leg up on the oak log that served as a chopping block. "I could count the butts and empty bottles 'round the pond to prove it!"

"You see me trying to deny it?" I asked, leaning against the tractor. "The pond was about the only place I could go where it was quiet. I didn't have to worry with Robert and I could sneak a smoke."

J.T. and I had been smoking cornstalks since I was nine or ten and smoking cigarettes since I was twelve. And sometimes J.T. would bring a bottle or two of beer he'd snuck out of his Daddy's truck. The beer was always warm, but we didn't care.

Even though Corinthia and Little George knew I was bumming cigarettes off Cotton, Granny and Paw Paw never seemed to suspect. Granny could still pick up the scent of her roses, but she didn't notice the smoky smell on my clothes. If Robert ever saw me with a cigarette, I'd bribe him to keep his mouth shut by giving him a couple of drags. We taught him how to blow smoke rings, and he enjoyed a cigarette even more than I did.

"I can't go fishin' today." Cotton reached in his pocket for his Camels. "I gotta put some new plugs in this engine. And I gonna play some ball this afternoon." After he struck a match on the sole of his shoe and lit up, he offered me a cigarette.

"So how much are spark plugs?" I asked, checking over my shoulder to make sure Granny and Paw Paw weren't around as I inhaled.

"Gordy likely got some plugs layin' 'round," said Cotton. "He got all kinda tires and crap in that shop. And out back he got more junk—fenders and ol' wrecks with weeds growin' through the engines and floorboards."

"You ever see any Cushman scooters?"

"Naw, but I keeps my eyes open for you."

"I want to buy that used one from Mr. Jenkins in town. He's got it in the shed behind the hardware store."

"I seed it back there. How it run?"

"I've never had it out. It might need some new tires, but it's supposed to get about 60 miles to the gallon."

"Before you buys it, I look it over. I knows more 'bout engines than mosta the white mens at Gordy's, but you sure wouldn't know it by what he pay me."

"Gordy's ain't the only garage in the county."

"Yeah, but some mens don't like to hire colored. And most mens don't like settin' at a card table with colored."

"Maybe they just don't like to lose." I envied Cotton's easy confidence and card-playing ability. "I've heard folks say you're so lucky you could climb a tall pine and shit in a swinging bucket."

"Don't know 'bout that, but I been messin' with cards longer than I been messin' with engines. And I always takes my rabbit's foot and my ice pick."

"Your ice pick?"

"Yes, suh. I never goes to Gordy's without it. There lotsa mens I don't know goin' in and outa that back room that ain't farmers. They playin' for big money."

"You ever play with Alvin Earl?"

"Not if I can help it." He snubbed out his cigarette in the dirt. "No one like to play with him."

"Why not?"

"When he lose—and he lose a lot—he get real mad and calls folks cheaters. And when he drinkin', he gots a real bad temper."

"He's got a bad temper even when he ain't drinking."

8

After I finished weeding the rose beds later that morning, I went into the kitchen. I scooped up some water from the sink and splashed it on the back of my neck, letting it trickle down my shoulders. Granny came in and gave me a glass of cold tea. Then she handed me a brand new quarter.

"I got this at the bank." Giving me a slight smile, she said, "You can add this to your savings."

"Thanks." I took a big swallow of tea and examined the picture of Washington on the face. After I wiped my mouth off, I tucked the coin in my pocket. "I almost have enough money to buy that used scooter in town."

"You've been saving up a long time for that scooter, and I appreciate all your hard work in my garden. You know, your mother carried roses from those beds when she was married."

Nodding, I headed toward the bedroom and glanced at my parents' wedding picture on Granny's piano. I didn't have many memories of my parents or my father's parents. They died before I was born. And Granny didn't like to talk about my mother or the accident—she said it was too painful.

When I opened the door, I saw Robert huddled in the corner. He had my composition notebook with the marble cover on his lap and something shiny in his hand. When I moved closer to see what it was, he shoved it in his pocket.

"Hey, you're supposed to be helping me in Granny's garden. What are you doing in here with my notebook?"

Robert jerked his head toward the wall and acted like he didn't hear me.

"I'm not playing around. I know you hear me. Give me my notebook and show me what you've got in your hand."

Robert turned back around. He lowered his eyes as he slowly pulled out a wad of lined paper and my mother's fountain pen from his pocket.

"Where'd you get my pen?" I reached for it, but he stuck it back in his pocket.

"I'm doing my schoolwork." As he unfolded the crumpled paper, I saw the ink stains on his fingers. His printing looked like something done by a six-year-old with a big, fat pencil. "It says *Robert and Lucas*. I wrote it all by myself."

"I know you did, but I don't like you messing with my stuff. That pen belonged to my mother."

"Lizba? She's in heaven with your daddy and the angels." He made it sound like my mother had gone shopping in Crisscross for the morning.

I'd never heard Robert mention her or call her by name. Kneeling next to him, I touched his arm. "Do you remember anything about her before she went to heaven?"

Robert blinked a couple of times and picked at the mole on his elbow. "I didn't want her to go." Then he looked at me and asked, "Can I write my name again?"

"No, quit messing with that mole and tell me about your sister—Elizabeth. You called her Lizba and she called you Bobby. She gave you your Pooh Bear for Christmas one year."

Still picking at his mole, he gazed out the window and started humming "Jesus Loves Me." I straightened up and put my notebook on the dresser. I knew there was no use trying to talk with him. "You're just like Granny. You remember what you want to remember. If Lizba had given you a new quarter or some Juicy Fruit gum, I bet you could tell me all about her."

As soon as I said "Juicy Fruit," I got his attention. He smiled, bobbing his head up and down like a wind-up toy. "You like anything sweet. I bet you'd pick up a sucker that somebody threw on the ground and lick it."

"No, no, that's nasty." He wrinkled his nose and stuck out his chin.

"It's real nasty. But if you give me back my pen," I bargained, "we'll play cowboys and Indians out in the yard. You can get out your cap gun."

"Yippee!" he shouted. Pulling the pen out of his pocket, he stood up and shoved it into my hand.

While Robert searched through his bottom drawer, trying to find his little silver gun, I pulled out my quarter. I rolled the coin through my fingers like the magician I'd seen at one of the county fairs. But even though I'd been practicing, I dropped it a couple of times. The second time it fell, Robert stooped down and grabbed it, sliding his thumb back and forth across the smooth surface.

"Lucas, I don't want to play cowboys and Indians. Let's play the money game."

"All right, give me my quarter back." I closed the door and pulled open my desk drawer. As soon as I picked up my money sock, I could tell it was lighter than usual. I quickly counted out the coins on my bed. I was missing more than four dollars—almost half my savings. Yanking the drawer out of the desk, I dumped everything on the floor.

"What are you doing?" Robert asked, keeping his eye on the piles.

"Some of my scooter money is gone. Did you take anything out of my sock to buy some candy?"

"No." Robert couldn't lie even if he wanted to. He'd shift his eyes toward the ground and pick at his mole or pull on his ear. Sometimes, if he was really nervous, he'd pull on both ears. Sticking his hand in his pocket, he offered me the coin he always carried. "You want my lucky penny? You can have it."

"No, no. Little George gave you that penny."

Looking relieved, Robert put the coin back in his pocket and gave it a little pat.

"Someone's taken a lot more than a penny out of my sock." Even if Robert might try to count my money, I knew he wouldn't take any of it. I went into the kitchen and asked Granny if she had taken any of my money. She was rinsing some dishes in the sink, and at first I wasn't sure she heard me.

"Did you take any money out of my drawer?" I asked in a loud voice.

"No, I wouldn't take your money." She cut off the water and slowly turned to face me with a dish towel and glass in her hand. "Did you take it to school?"

"No ma'am. Why would I take it to school?"

"Did you check to see if some of the money had fallen behind your desk?"

"I even pulled the drawer out and looked under the desk. More than four dollars is gone! No one knows where I hide it except you and Robert."

"Corinthia probably knows, but she would never take it."

"Alvin Earl—he's the only other person who's been in the house. That son of a bitch took my scooter money to buy whiskey and gamble."

"Watch your language, Lucas." She reached for the thick bar of soap on the sink. "I can still wash your mouth out."

"I'm not nine years old anymore." I pointed my finger at her and said slowly, "Alvin Earl took my money just like he took my Walking Liberty half dollar when I was in the fourth grade. And you know it."

I'd found the fifty-cent piece in the parking lot at the fairground. It had a mint mark from 1937, and Little George told me it was probably almost pure silver. I scrubbed it with an old toothbrush to make it look nice and shiny. Then I put it on the back porch table to dry, and the next day it was gone. Alvin Earl said one of the pickers likely stuck it in their pocket when they took a water break. But I figured it was likely in his pocket.

"I'd forgotten about your half dollar," she said, trailing her fingers across the soap.

"I didn't. And I still think Alvin Earl took it."

She hesitated for a second. "I'm missing some money from my Lottie Moon offering box and a pair of sapphire earrings my mother gave me on my twenty-fifth birthday. I thought I'd misplaced them."

"He stole your church money and jewelry?" I couldn't believe Alvin Earl would even steal from Granny. "That's pretty low. Did you say anything to him?"

"Oh, no. I don't want to accuse him when I'm not sure he took them."

"Who else would have taken them? And who else would take my money? He just thought I wouldn't notice," I shouted, flinging my arms in the air.

"There's no need to yell, Lucas."

"He's a thief," I hollered, slamming my fist on the table. "Did you say anything to Paw Paw?"

She shook her head. "I don't want to upset him now that he's having all these heart problems. And I don't want you saying anything to him either."

"Half my scooter money is gone. Do you know how long I've been saving up to buy that motor scooter?"

"I'll say something to Paw Paw when the time is right."

"When the time is right?" I exploded. "What does that mean?"

"I'll say something to Paw Paw as soon as he feels better and I know it was definitely Alvin Earl."

"Well, you better keep your jewelry locked up and hide your offering box. Even if Paw Paw feels better, the time's never going to be right as long as Alvin Earl's around!"

9

Paw Paw worked in the fields all day, but he said he felt good that night. After supper, we all sat out on the front porch. As the sun went down, he parked himself on the swing and cleaned his shotgun. Robert ran around the yard trying to catch fireflies. And I claimed my regular spot on the steps and listened to the Red Sox game.

"This gun belonged to my daddy and I want to take good care of it," Paw Paw said, rubbing the wooden stock with a soft rag. "Quail season will be here before you know it."

"I heard a couple of bobwhites out near the barn today," said Granny from the rocker.

"Sam and I will be ready." Paw Paw peered through the sight on the tip of the barrel.

There were lots of birds and deer in the backwoods on our property. But I didn't care anything about hunting or killing a buck for an antler trophy. I didn't like to shoot any kind of animal except the wild boars that tore up the garden. And I hated to clean the quail when their bodies were still warm.

While Paw Paw talked about all the birds he wanted to bring down this season, I hoped Granny would say something about my missing money or her missing jewelry. But she didn't say a word about either one. Instead, she turned to me and asked, "Do you have all your homework done?"

"Almost," I said, despite the fact that I hadn't started my history or math assignments. "Can Little George take me to school tomorrow?"

"No, there's still a lot of fieldwork to do," Paw Paw said. "You'll have to take the bus."

"When I get my scooter, I won't have to get up so early and ride that bus," I said.

"I know you miss riding with James Thomas," Granny said. "But you need to make some new friends now that the Ledbetters have gone back to Albany."

Even though there were other kids at school who liked to fish and smoke, I knew I'd never find a friend as good as J.T. We'd been buddies since the fifth grade and rode the same bus. Sometimes we'd walk home together, always stopping at the Crisscross water tower at the edge of town to have a quick cigarette. I sat next to him in homeroom and most of my classes. He was the star algebra student and wanted to go to Georgia Tech. He helped me with my algebra, and sometimes I helped him with his essays.

His daddy was a tenant farmer and worked the place next to ours. J.T. didn't talk much about it, but I knew his daddy drank and didn't have much luck growing cotton or anything else. He wasn't a mean drunk like Alvin Earl, and he'd never hit J.T. or his mother. But he'd go out and do crazy things, like buying J.T.'s little sister a pair of lace-up roller skates or bringing home a fur coat for his mother to wear on the farm. And sometimes he'd get real sad thinking about his younger brother who'd been killed at Normandy and cry for hours.

Last fall, a few weeks after school started, he sat on the porch and cried for two days. While he drank his whiskey, he rambled on about paying his grocery bills and missing his little brother. Mrs. Ledbetter couldn't get him to come in the house to eat or sleep. When he finally got up, he disappeared in the nearby woods with his rifle and a bottle. J.T. and I spent most of the weekend looking for him.

That next Monday, J.T. wasn't at school, and I had a bad feeling about his daddy. As soon as the last bell rang, I picked up J.T.'s assignments and headed to the bus. When I got home, Robert was out in the chicken coop with Corinthia, and Granny and Paw Paw were sitting at the kitchen table waiting for me. Glancing at their faces, I knew something terrible had happened.

"Come sit down, Lucas." Granny patted the chair next to her.

I swallowed hard and shook my head. I wanted to stand in case I had to brace myself.

Paw Paw stood up and shifted his weight from one foot to the other. "We got a call from Sheriff Norton after lunch. They found J.T.'s daddy's body in the creek under the railway trestle—he had a broken neck."

"He fell off the trestle?" I gripped the back of a chair. Imagining the narrow strip of wooden ties that stretched at least fifty feet above the creek made me dizzy.

"Well, he…"

But before Granny could finish, Paw Paw interrupted. "Tell him the truth, Lettie. He's got a right to know what happened."

"Sheriff Norton thinks he jumped off the trestle," Granny said slowly. "He'd been dead a couple of days when they found him."

"Jumped? What are you talking about?" I was shaking so bad I could barely get the words out.

"The sheriff found his rifle along with his wallet on the tracks." She brushed an invisible crumb off the table.

"But why? I don't understand."

"That man just wasn't cut out to farm." Paw Paw rubbed his chin with the back of his hand. "He couldn't catch on and break even. Maybe Little George and I should have tried to help him more."

"After he lost his younger brother a few years back, he just didn't seem to have much interest in farming or anything else." Granny's voice trailed off.

I was shocked. I couldn't believe anyone would jump off the trestle. And I shivered when I pictured Mr. Ledbetter sailing through the air and slamming into the dried-out creek bed filled with rocks and dead branches.

There'd never been a suicide in Crisscross that I knew about, and I tried to make some sense of what had happened. Granny said suicides ran in J.T.'s daddy's family and that his daddy's daddy had shot himself. But part of me still wanted to think Mr. Ledbetter must have fallen off the bridge because he was so drunk. A week earlier, J.T. and I had been tossing a baseball around in their yard. His daddy had been joking around with us about watching out for pretty girls and telling J.T. he was going to be the best pitcher on the high school team.

"The church took up a collection so Mrs. Ledbetter can ship his body back to Albany and help with the burial," said Granny. "I don't think he had much insurance."

"Do you think they'll have an open casket?" I asked. I didn't remember my parents' funeral and hadn't seen many dead people since Mr. Terrell, our old postman, had died a couple years ago.

"Hell no, Lucas!" Paw Paw said. "No one in their right mind would want to look at anyone who's jumped off a trestle. Why would you ask something like that?"

"I don't know," I said, stung by his question.

"I just hope for the children's sake that their preacher can find something good to say about their daddy," said Granny, patting me on the shoulder.

"Well, he'd better. Ledbetteter was a good man. And it ain't the preacher's job or anybody else's to judge," Paw Paw said as he went out onto the back porch.

The next day, J.T. came by the house to tell me they were moving to Albany to live with his aunt. I helped him load up their furniture in his daddy's old pickup. I told him I was real sorry about what happened, but J.T. never mentioned his daddy or shed a tear.

After he moved, I wrote him a short letter. Granny said I shouldn't expect an answer since he was probably trying to put everything that happened at Crisscross behind him. But I figured there was no way he could ever forget about his daddy jumping off that bridge.

I couldn't. I had the same dream about falling off a cliff night after night for the next few weeks. I'd be standing on an overlook high above a rushing river as it was getting dark. I'd stumble and try to grab onto a tree or root. But the trees slipped through my hands, and the roots snapped like quail bones when I was cleaning a dead bird. I'd feel myself falling and scream for help. But no one was around—I was all alone. Just before I was going to hit the water, I'd wake up twisted in my sheets, breathing hard and covered in sweat. It took me a couple of minutes to remember where I was. And I wondered if anyone heard me scream.

10

Robert knew the Ledbetters had moved, but no one ever told him why. We didn't talk about Mr. Ledbetter's suicide or the family's sudden decision to go to back to Albany. But I thought about them every time I passed their boarded-up house and overgrown fields. And I wondered if I'd ever see J.T. again.

45

Even though I never said anything, Robert knew I missed going to school with my friend and fishing with him at the pond. He could barely count to ten, but he was real good about picking up on folks' feelings. And he picked up on my sadness.

One day when I was helping Cotton work on the tractor, he came out to the shed. Looking at all the wrenches and tools scattered around the sawhorses, he said, "What are y'all doing?"

"Just tryin' to get this ol' tractor runnin'," said Cotton, twisting his head around to look at him. "You wanna help?"

"Yeah." Squirming like a little kid who needed to pee, Robert slid his hand into his overalls pocket.

"You got something in your pocket?" I asked.

"A surprise," he said with a sly smile.

"A surprise?" asked Cotton. "Today somebody's birthday?"

"No. But it's something y'all are going to like." Robert giggled. "Now close your eyes and put out your hand."

Closing his eyes, Cotton stuck out his hand. "You better not put a frog in it. I hates frogs. They gives you warts."

"It's not a frog." Robert giggled again. "Close your eyes, Lucas."

"It's too hot to be messing around. Just tell us what it is." I took off my cap and wiped my face.

Cotton poked me. "Come on. Let him have some fun."

"All right, all right." I squinted at Robert and stuck out my hand.

"No peeking." He pulled something that looked like a pencil stub from his pocket.

"Can we open our eyes now?" I fingered the long, thin object in my palm.

"Yeah—look at your surprise."

46

Opening my eyes wide, I saw a cigarette in my hand and a cigarette in Cotton's hand. "Where did you get these?"

Robert stared at the toe of his shoe. "From Alvin Earl."

"Alvin Earl?" Cotton snorted. "He wouldn't give a cigarette to a dyin' soldier, much less you."

"You took them out of his pack, didn't you?" I asked.

Robert shook his head and smiled. "No, I borrowed them."

"You know you can't smoke a cigarette and then give it back. It ain't like borrowing someone's pencil," I said. "Where'd you find them?"

"On the table." He pointed to the back porch. "Are you mad at me?"

"We've talked about this before," I said slowly. "You can't mess around with folks' stuff. And you can't borrow cigarettes from Alvin Earl or anyone else."

"That gets you in trouble," said Cotton.

"Yeah, real big trouble." I glanced over my shoulder to make sure no one was on the back porch watching us. Then I grabbed the cigarette out of Cotton's hand.

"What you gonna do?" asked Cotton.

"I'm going to slip these back in Alvin Earl's pack before he notices they're gone."

"If you really wants a smoke, Robert, ask me," said Cotton. "Just don't ask me when Miz Lettie 'round. She like to have a fit."

"She'd tell Paw Paw to fire you if she knew you were giving him cigarettes," I said.

"Well, I might not be 'round here much longer."

"Where you going?" asked Robert.

"I been thinkin' 'bout headin' up north to find some work."

"You don't think you can get a job in the South?"

"Yeah, I can get a job. Any colored man can get a job makin' nickels and dimes. But I don't wanna spend the resta my life pickin' cotton or sweepin' out a garage sayin' 'yes, suh'; 'right away, suh' all day. I wants a job with some future."

"You think you can do better up north?"

"I gots to give it a try, Lucas." Cotton looked at me for a while and then said, "I don't wanna end up like Cordelle."

"Cordelle? You mean Digger?" He was about Cotton's age and worked at Duncan's Funeral Home digging graves and burying people. He lived in an old shack with newspapers stuck in the windows in the colored section of Crisscross. And he had at least one, maybe two, little kids with a woman from Macon.

"Yeah, his real name Cordelle. He hold the home run record in high school, probably still do. Coach say he could hit a ball a country mile. But he gonna spend his whole life pushin' a shovel."

"It's honest work and somebody's got to do it."

"Well, it ain't gonna be me." Reaching for his glove, Cotton curled his fist and massaged the leather with his knuckles. "I gonna try and play some ball on one of the big teams. Nothin' holdin me here. Ain't got no land or much family."

"You got any family up there?"

"My momma got a cousin workin' in a factory in Cleveland. He got a nice car—not some beat up ol' truck with a bad muffler and a leaky radiator—and he savin' up to buy a house."

"You can buy a house around here and probably get it for a good price. Little George's got a nice little house."

"Yeah, Little George has a real nice house," echoed Robert.

"But I wanna house with indoor plumbing and electricity. If I ever tries to buy a nice house 'round here, white folks be callin' me uppity and tellin' me to go on back where I belongs. Some folks might do somethin' worse than that."

"Did you say anything to Little George and Corinthia?" I asked, hoping they might convince him to stay in Crisscross.

"They don't wanna see me go. But even if I don't play ball, they knows I can fin' more work up north."

"When are you thinking about going?"

"I ain't sure. I gotta get some money saved up."

I didn't say anything, but I knew I'd hate to see him go, especially since J.T. had moved. I didn't want to lose two friends in less than a year.

## 11

With J.T. gone and Cotton talking about leaving, I wasn't sure what I wanted to do. Alvin Earl kept nagging Paw Paw to make me work on the farm full-time, but Granny wouldn't hear of my dropping out of school. She wanted me to make something of myself. I didn't like math and wasn't sure if I wanted to go to college. But I knew I didn't want to spend the rest of my life spreading fertilizer and picking cotton.

I dreaded the days I had to ride the bus if Carlton and George Overton, the twins who lived down the road from us, were on board. Robert always stood by the mailbox with me, waiting for the bus in the mornings. Granny kept him on the farm most of the time, but everyone in town knew him. He was kind of like the local freak. When the twins and their younger brother were on the bus, they started screaming as soon as they saw him. Carlton and George would press their faces against the windows and yell, "Hey, Robert! Look at us! We could be your twin."

They were the tallest boys in the class and looked exactly alike, except for the splotchy purple mark on George's neck. Granny said I should feel sorry for them because their mother died when they were young. They lived in a run-down house with broken windows and more rusted-out ice boxes and washers in their yard than the Crisscross dump. They always had a couple of mangy-looking dogs roaming around their property and a mean old rooster that would peck your eyes out if you got too close to the front porch.

But even though they didn't have a mother and their daddy spent a lot of time at Gordy's, it was hard to feel sorry for them. Corinthia called them white trash and said they were probably going to end up in reform school. I'd done some things I wasn't real proud of like dropping a cat in a tub of water to see if it could swim. But I'd seen the twins pack kittens in the dirt and then run over their heads with a lawn mower. They stole things out of kids' lockers, and I was pretty sure they took the missing picture money from our homeroom teacher's desk earlier this year.

As soon as I stepped on the bus that morning, Carlton sprang out of his seat. "Hey, Lucas, where's that crazy Robert?"

"How come Flat Face never went to school?" George asked in a hard voice.

"Yeah, how come?" echoed Donald, their little brother.

I sprinted down the aisle and found a middle seat while Mr. Nelson, the driver, hunched over the steering wheel and picked at his fingernails. I hoped he would say something to the boys. But he never did. They followed me and parked themselves right across the aisle from me. I sank into the window seat, wishing I could disappear.

"My brother asked you a question and you'd better answer him," said Carlton, leaning so close to me that I could smell his sour breath. "How come your uncle never went to school? Maybe we should report him to the truant officer."

George cut in. "Oh, I forgot. They never had classes for kids that drooled and weren't right in the head in Crisscross."

"They sent them off to the state hospital with all the other crazy people," said Carlton. "When you going to send your uncle to Maysville?" His eyes flashed, daring me to say something back or try to defend Robert.

If J.T. were with me, he would have said, "Shut up! Mind your own business!" or something a lot worse. And even though I hated having a mongoloid uncle who could barely speak, I would have said, "Yeah, lay off Robert and leave me alone!"

J.T. had a lot more guts than I did. He wouldn't take any crap off the Overtons or anyone else. But when the Ledbetters packed up to go to Albany, J.T. took my courage with him. And I didn't want any trouble since I was all alone now.

As the bus crept along, I acted like I didn't hear them, concentrating real hard on looking out the window. I thought about riding my scooter to Albany to go fishing and smoke a few cigarettes with my old friend. I didn't want to give these boys the satisfaction of knowing they were getting to me.

Once we got closer to school and passed the water tower and the Brown's roadside produce stand, Mr. Nelson started to pick up the other kids. The brothers got bored with their game and forgot about Robert. I wished I could forget about him, too.

When I got to school, I headed for the library. The Overtons never went to the library, and it was the only place in the building that didn't smell like Clorox, old socks, and pee.

"Morning, Lucas," said Mrs. Jenkins, the librarian who'd been at the school when my mother was a student. "Have you finished the book on baseball greats?"

"Yes, ma'am." I handed her my book. "Now I need something for my book report, but it has to be fiction."

"I've got a brand new bestseller about a very valuable collie that lives in England. Do you have a dog?"

"We've got some stray cats, and my granddad has a bird dog named Samson."

"Oh, Samson. Everyone in Crisscross knows about Sam. Folks say he's the best bird dog in the county."

"Maybe. Some big banker from Columbus wanted to buy him for $400 a couple of years ago. But Paw Paw didn't want to sell him."

"I remember hearing something about that. Do you hunt?"

"No. I can eat quail, but I hate cleaning them."

"Well, I know you'll take good care of this new book. Your mother always took good care of her books. She liked to read as much as you do."

"What did she read?"

"Everything—she wanted to read her way through the library and become a writer."

"A writer? I never knew that." I wondered what my mother would think if she knew that I liked to write, too.

"Yes, she wanted to work for a newspaper. Now you better get to class."

I headed to my homeroom with Miss Gilbert, a middle-aged woman with big bosoms and little brown hairs on her upper lip. When I got there, I saw a new student who looked like she should be in the sixth grade sitting by her desk. She was small and skinny with long dark hair and eyes that reminded me of a young doe. All the kids stared at her as they filed to their seats, but she didn't seem to notice.

The bell rang and a wet glob hit me right below my ear. As I rubbed my neck with the back of my hand, I heard Carlton whisper in a voice loud enough for everyone to hear, "Bull's-eye!" George let out a mean laugh when a little wad of paper covered with spit fell to the floor.

Ignoring the twins, Miss Gilbert wrote the date on the board and rapped on her desk with a ruler. "That was the first bell, class. Let's get settled down. Who wants to lead us in the Pledge and the Lord's Prayer today?"

I was still scrubbing my neck when Marshall Thompson, one of the biggest suck-ups in the building, stuck his hand in Miss Gilbert's face. He lived in a big house in Crisscross and his daddy worked for the county offices. Marshall always wore ironed shirts and Sunday shoes. But I could still remember when we were six years old and he wet his pants on the first day of school. He started crying so hard that Miss Waldrip, our teacher, had to call his mother to come and get him.

"I'll do it, ma'am," he said.

Miss Gilbert nodded at Marshall, and we quickly recited the pledge and the prayer. As soon as we finished, she said, "We've got a new student in our class today and she's going to introduce herself."

Even the Overtons got quiet and turned to look at the girl in the red and blue plaid jumper. None of the other girls wore velvet ribbons or jumpers to school, and I could hear them snickering about her clothing. The new girl pretended she didn't hear them. And even though she wasn't pretty, there was something about her face that made me pay attention to what she was going to say.

She stood up and said in a loud voice, "My name is Amelia Weinstein, and I'm from New York."

"Amelia Weinstein?" hooted Carlton. "What kind of a name is that?"

"I'm named for Amelia Earhart, the pilot."

"Who?" George called out.

"Now class, let's raise our hands," said Miss Gilbert.

"In case you haven't heard, she was the first woman to fly across the Atlantic," said Amelia. "And she got the Distinguished Flying Cross." She spoke really fast and sounded like she didn't have time to answer any stupid questions from the Overton twins or anyone else.

Nobody was very impressed with Amelia Earhart's award. But Emily Anne Morris, the preacher's daughter and another suck-up, waved her hand in the air and announced, "Miss Earhart wrote a couple of books, too." She paused long enough to make sure everyone heard her. "They're in the library."

Emily Anne had long blonde hair and boobs almost as big as Miss Gilbert's. J.T. and I used to watch the girls' PE class so we could see her boobs bouncing up and down under her green gym suit. J.T. always said he'd pay a thousand dollars if he could touch just one for three seconds. But I didn't like her know-it-all attitude and never wanted to get that close to her.

Miss Gilbert smiled at Emily Anne as if she were the smartest student in the building. Then, turning toward Amelia, she asked, "Do you live in town?"

"Yes, I'm staying with my grandmother, Caroline Newsom."

"Oh, I know Caroline, and I remember your mother. She was the valedictorian of her class and then went to Emory, didn't she?"

Amelia blushed slightly and nodded.

"You can take James Thomas's old desk in the back of the room."

She pointed toward the empty seat next to me and said, "Lucas, please share your books with Amelia until I can get a set from the principal. Show her the information about our book report."

"Yes, ma'am," I said, barely moving my lips. I kept my eyes on the new girl marching down the aisle.

"Now share your books with Amelia, Lucas," George snickered. "She's going to be in the top of the class."

"Yeah, she might be even smarter than your Uncle Robert. And she doesn't drool." Carlton cracked his knuckles and deliberately stuck his foot out in the aisle.

"Watch out!" I said as Amelia headed towards the empty desk.

Amelia's eyes shifted toward me for half a second. Then she shot Carlton a hateful glance. "Move your boot."

"Oh, sorry," said Carlton in a mocking tone as he pulled his foot back. "I didn't see you coming."

I was surprised when Carlton moved his foot. I'd never heard a student order the twins to do anything. Even some of the teachers were afraid of them.

Amelia sat down and smoothed out her jumper without looking my way.

"This tells you about the report. I hope you can read it." I handed her the book report information I'd copied off the board. "You can take it home if you want."

She took my notes but didn't speak to me until we got ready to change classes. She noticed my library book and whispered, "They made a movie out of that book."

"You don't see many collies around here," I said.

"I wouldn't know. And I hope I'm not here long enough to find out."

"Are you moving?"

"I'm going back to New York."

I didn't say anything, but I wished I could move, too.

### 12

I had a couple of classes with Amelia, but she didn't speak to me or anyone else for the next couple of weeks. She took careful notes in class, and if a teacher called on her, she always had the right answer. But she never raised her hand to ask a question or volunteer.

When we changed classes, she walked by herself, clutching her books and light blue pencil box close to her chest. Some of the girls giggled about the jumpers she wore every day, but she kept her eyes straight ahead, passing through the halls as if she were the only one in the building. During lunch she sat alone at a small table stuck in the corner of the cafeteria and read a library book or sketched on notebook paper.

On her first day of school, she'd tried to sit in an empty chair at Emily Anne's lunch table. Emily Anne was the most popular girl in our class, and all the girls claimed a chair at her table early in the year. They piled their books and sweaters on the empty chair. And I heard Emily Anne say Amelia talked funny because she was from up north and her father was Jewish.

When Amelia pulled out the empty chair, Emily Anne put her hand on the back of it and said loud and clear, "Somebody's sitting here and she's a Christian from Georgia."

Staring at the empty spot, Amelia asked in a cool voice, "Has she ever heard of the Golden Rule?" Then she turned her back and walked toward the corner of the cafeteria with her head held high.

"Who does she think she is?" demanded one of the other girls at Emily Anne's table. She threw a couple of sandwich crusts at Amelia's back. The other girls cackled like old hens when the strips of bread hit her jumper. I felt kind of sorry for her, but I knew better than to say anything.

After lunch each day, Amelia would rush out of the cafeteria and head to Mr. Goodman's history class, one of the classes we had together. When she took her assigned seat, the other kids pulled their chairs away from her as if she had some kind of disease. I didn't pull my chair away, but I didn't try to speak to her either. I looked at her sideways while I pretended to listen to Mr. Goodman's long, boring lectures and took notes.

History was our last class of the day, and the building was always hot and clammy by noon. Even with Amelia sitting next to me, I counted down the minutes until dismissal.

Mr. Goodman was a direct descendant of General John B. Gordon, a Civil War hero who went on to become state governor. No matter what we were supposed to be studying, he talked about the War of Northern Aggression. He told lots of corny jokes and covered the blackboard with diagrams of troop movements and arrows going every which way. We could never get beyond Lee's surrender at Appomattox Courthouse and Reconstruction.

One day when kids were even drowsier than usual and even Amelia seemed bored, Mr. Goodman said, "Wake up! We've been talking about the carpetbaggers and scalawags for three days. I'm giving y'all a pop quiz."

Everyone groaned except Amelia. She took out a sheet of paper and pulled a yellow pencil out of her little case. But the point was broken. I heard her say something to herself about not having another pencil in her blue case.

Without looking at her, I put my only extra pencil on her desk. She immediately handed it back to me and whispered, "I don't want it. I'll use a pen."

"Take it," I said, sounding like I was giving her an order. "I don't need it."

"All right." She flipped through her notes and avoided looking at me.

The next morning she barely gave me a nod in homeroom. When I tried to catch her eye in history class, she studied her notes as if she were getting ready for a college exam. She wouldn't look at me for the rest of the week. I thought I must have made her mad when I gave her the pencil. Right after the final bell rang the next Friday, she stuck a folded piece of paper in my hand. "Here's a picture," she said.

"A picture?" Unfolding the paper, I saw a colored sketch of a collie with long hair and a collar. "It looks just like Lassie."

Giving me a tiny smile, she said quickly, "I want to go to art school when I graduate."

"Art school?" I asked.

"Yes, and then I want to live in New York and do something that people will remember."

I didn't know what to say. I knew I didn't want to work on the farm when I graduated—I wanted to travel and see both the Atlantic and Pacific Oceans, but I wasn't sure what I wanted to do.

I gathered up my books and looked at her sketch again. "Your drawing is real good. Thanks." Except for a crumpled-up Valentine I'd gotten from Emily Anne in fourth grade, it was the first thing a girl had ever given me. I wondered if Amelia had given drawings to any of the other boys she'd known.

When I got home, I showed Robert the sketch. I told him about Amelia and the story of how Lassie tried to find his way back to his master.

"Is Amelia your girlfriend?" he asked, more interested in Amelia than in Lassie.

"No, she's just a new girl that sits next to me." I carefully folded the sketch and tucked it in the back of my composition notebook. I wanted to keep it close by so I could look at it.

"Lucas has a girlfriend. Lucas has a girlfriend," he sang, jumping around the room.

"Shut up, Robert. I hardly even know her."

## 13

Early the next Saturday morning, Granny Lettie and Paw Paw went into Crisscross to go to the bank. Little George was out in the fields, and Corinthia was on the porch sweeping cobwebs out of the ceiling corners with her broom. I was just finishing breakfast when Alvin Earl roared into the yard in his truck.

He got out and hurried onto the porch. "You seen my lighter, Corinthia?"

"No, but I remembers it, Mr. Alvin Earl." She stuck her broom in a corner. "Your lucky lighter got that fancy one-eyed Jack on it—right?"

"Yep, you'll never see another one like it." He burst into the kitchen and asked, "You seen it, Lucas?"

I shook my head.

"It could have fallen out of my pocket when I was sitting on the porch talking to Daddy the other night." He shoved a biscuit in his mouth.

"I doin' laundry this morning," Corinthia said from the doorway. "But if I sees it, I keeps it for you. Maybe it bring me some luck, too."

"You keep your eyes open." Alvin Earl strode out of the kitchen. He slammed the screen door behind him and took off in his truck.

"Well, thanks to you, mister," Corinthia muttered as he drove off. "Someone need to teach that man some manners." Turning to me she said, "Your grandmomma 'spectin' y'all to work in the garden this mornin'. Robert be out when he get outa the bathroom."

"It's going to be a hot one today." I stood up and grabbed my cap.

Corinthia fanned herself with her apron. "For sure, and it ain't even May. I gonna hang some clothes on the line."

I headed out to the pump house to fill the watering cans. After I filled them for the third time, I called to Corinthia, "Where's Robert? He's supposed to be out here, too. Is he still in the bathroom?"

She stretched a quilt out on the line and said, "Go tell him he need to get out here."

I had a pretty good idea what Robert was doing in the bathroom and figured Corinthia did, too. But I put down the hose and walked toward the house.

"Hurry up now, Lucas," she called. "Your grandmomma want you to get that waterin' done 'fore she get home."

I pulled open the screen door and hollered, "Robert, what are you doing in here? Come out and help me in the garden." The bathroom door was wide open, but I didn't see him. Then I noticed that our bedroom door was shut, and I smelled something burning. "Robert, are you in there?"

I pushed the door open and a gust of smoke poured out. The room felt hot enough to peel my skin off. Flames ripped along Robert's bed and rushed toward the ceiling. Stunned by the heat and smoke, I threw my arm over my mouth as I went in the room.

"Robert, where are you? Are you in here?" I shouted.

I heard kind of a gurgling sound and flung open the closet door. He was curled up in the corner, pressing an old tee-shirt to his face.

"Come on, Robert, you got to get out of there."

"No, no. There's a fire."

"You got to get out." Smoke stung my eyes and scalded my throat. My lungs burned. "It ain't safe in here!" I yanked his arm and somehow managed to pull him up.

Half pushing, half dragging, I got him out of the closet and into the kitchen. I gasped for a breath and pulled him out to the porch. Sucking in the fresh air, I finally got him to the yard. He fell down on the grass, coughing his guts out. And I rang the old field workers' bell as hard as I could.

"Fire, fire—there's a fire in the bedroom!"

"Sweet Jesus," Corinthia shrieked. "Robert all right?"

"Yeah," I said. "But the whole room's going up."

"Lord, help us," she said. "Get the buckets."

I grabbed a couple of the quilts off the line and rushed back in the house. Smoke poured out of the bedroom. I could barely see. Waving the smoke out of my face, I threw a quilt on Robert's bed as the flames shot up the window frame. Hot sparks fell on my hair and shirt, singeing my arms. I beat the curtains with the other quilt and heard the sound of breaking glass.

"Hurry!" I yelled. "Get some water!"

Sweat poured down my neck and chest. My tongue stuck to the roof of my mouth. I pounded the mattress with the quilt until the room shook. I fought for a breath of air while Corinthia passed me a dripping bucket. I slung water on the bed and wall. For a second, I thought the fire was out. But a row of flames sprang up along the headboard, sucking up the papers on my desk.

Grabbing another bucket from Robert, I shouted, "More water! Get more water!"

"Use the rug!" Corinthia yelled from the kitchen.

I snatched the rag rug off the bedroom floor and attacked the headboard and my desk. My arms ached from all the pounding. Watching the blazing pile of papers, I knew my sketch of Lassie would be ruined. But I couldn't stop. I hit the bed and desk until I could see only a few embers between the smoldering sheets. Robert's bear fell to the floor and bits of ash covered its fur. Jagged springs poked through the ticking like angry fingers pointing toward the scorched ceiling. Chunks of glass and blackened paper littered the floor. And tiny feathers floated around the room.

Looking up, I saw Little George in the doorway. I coughed and wiped the soot off my face with my arm.

"I heard the bell and got here as fast as I could," he said, surveying the room. "Looks like you gots it out and nobody hurt."

I rested my hands on my thighs, still feeling the heat from the flames. "Yeah, but there ain't much left. Look at my desk."

"Ain't much you could do 'bout that. Let's get all this mess outa here." He turned toward Corinthia. "Where that broom?"

We wadded up the soggy bedding and dragged it out, leaving a charred trail across the kitchen floor. Then we carried out what was left of my desk and the curtain shreds. "Watch out for all them little bitsa glass," said Little George.

Corinthia threw open all the windows. "Gotta get the smoke out—the whole house smell. Y'all gonna have to sleep on the porch tonight. Robert, go open the front door and then tell us what happen in there."

Robert stood by the front door, hanging his head like an old dog that had been whipped. He didn't want to talk to Corinthia or anyone else.

"How'd that fire start?" she demanded. "You playin' with some matches?"

Robert shook his head and tears pooled in his eyes.

"If Lucas hadn't come lookin' for you, you be trapped in there and burned to death!" she scolded.

"But you safe now," said Little George. "Tell us what happened."

"Tell us," I said.

Robert's eyes darted around the room, and he slowly pulled something shiny from his pants pocket.

"Alvin Earl's lighter!" I said, rubbing the sweat off my forehead with my arm. "You were playing with it on the bed, weren't you? What did I tell you about taking stuff that didn't belong to you?"

Robert shrugged and studied his shoe.

"Where'd you fin' it?" asked Little George, leaning on the broom.

Robert pointed to the couch in the parlor and turned toward the wall, too ashamed to look at us.

"Look at me." Corinthia snatched the lighter from his hand and stuck it in her apron pocket. "If you fin' somethin' that don't belong to you, you s'pose to give it back."

"Yeah, you know you don't mess around with stuff that ain't yours," I said. "Alvin Earl will tear you up when he finds out you had his lighter."

Backing into a corner, Robert covered his head with his hands.

"He won't be playin' with lighters no more," said Little George. "He know better now."

"He better not even look at that lighter or anything else that belongs to Alvin Earl. Now we've got to get the rest of this mess cleaned up," I said. "He's going to have some explaining to do."

## 14

Alvin Earl drove up to the house the next morning while Robert and I were finishing breakfast. He flung open the screen door and plowed into the kitchen. "I smell smoke. What the hell happened here?" he demanded, staring at the mound of torn bedding and tangled springs on the burn pile in the yard.

"There was a little fire in the bedroom, but we got it out," I said without looking at him.

Corinthia set out more biscuits. "They just outa the oven and I gots a fresh pot a coffee. You wants some, Mr. Alvin Earl?"

Shaking his head, Alvin Earl tore through the kitchen to the bedroom, taking in the broken windows and blackened walls. Soon he was back. "What do you mean a little fire? There's nothing left. That room's destroyed. Look at it."

"It got pretty hot in there, but no one got hurt," I said.

"That one-eyed jack real lucky," Corinthia said, handing him his lighter. "It better than a rabbit's foot."

Alvin Earl rubbed his thumb across the jack's face, flicking his eyes toward Robert. "That dimwit found my lighter and tried to burn the house down, didn't he?"

Robert sank down in his chair and ducked his head as if he were about to get hit.

"God watchin' out for those boys," Corinthia said. "He know Robert need lots of extra care."

Alvin Earl scowled. He shoved his finger in Robert's face. "That boy don't need care. He needs a lesson. And if Daddy can't give it to him, I will."

I was afraid what Alvin Earl might do to teach Robert a lesson. "Maybe you should leave your lighter in your truck. Granny doesn't like anyone smoking in the house," I said.

"Are you trying to tell me what I can and can't do?" he demanded.

Before I could say anything else, Granny came into the kitchen. Looking at Robert, she said, "We've talked about what happened yesterday, and Robert has something to say to you, don't you?"

Staring at the floor, he mumbled, "I'm sorry."

"Sorry for what?" prompted Granny.

"I'm sorry I took the lighter," he said.

"Stand up when you talk to me and quit mumbling," Alvin Earl ordered.

"I'm sorry I took the lighter," Robert repeated as he stood up and reached for Granny's hand. "I won't take it again."

"I can't understand a word you say. But I'll teach you a lesson you won't forget." Moving toward Robert, Alvin Earl yanked off his belt and snapped it in the air.

"What are you going to do?" I stood up, keeping my eyes on the leather strap.

"I'm going to wear him out." Alvin Earl wrapped the metal buckle around his fist.

"Oh, no." Granny planted herself in front of Robert like some kind of human shield. "You're not going to beat your brother."

"He didn't understand about lighters." I took a couple of quick steps toward Alvin Earl, knocking my chair over with a loud crash.

Corinthia picked up the chair and whispered, "Watch yourself now, Lucas. Don't get folks riled up."

"He's just like a dog." Alvin Earl moved closer to Robert. "Beating him is the only way he's going to remember anything."

"He's not a dog," I said. "You don't have to beat him."

"Shut your mouth before I shut it for you. This ain't any of your business," snapped Alvin Earl.

"What do you mean it's none of my business? I live here—I share a room with Robert," I shouted.

As Corinthia grabbed my arm, Paw Paw came into the kitchen. Struggling to get a breath, he said, "Leave the boys alone. I'll handle this."

"How are you going to handle it, Daddy?" pressed Alvin Earl, his belt buckle still wrapped around his hand. "You can barely make it out to the porch."

"I said I'll handle it," Paw Paw said in an irritated voice.

"He's so stupid—he'll forget about the fire tomorrow. He can't even remember where he lives."

"What did you say?" demanded Granny.

"You heard me. He's too stupid to remember anything," said Alvin Earl.

We all stared at Alvin Earl. And silence filled the air.

"I don't ever want to hear that word in this house," said Granny. "Do you understand?"

"Go on home and leave him be," said Paw Paw, holding on to the back of a chair for support. "I told you I'll take care of it."

Alvin Earl slammed the screen door and stormed across the yard. He got in his truck and tore out the drive.

Shaking his head, Paw Paw leaned against the wall. His face sagged, and he looked like someone had flattened him out with one of the county's road graders.

"Let me help you back into the bedroom, Paw Paw," I said. "And you can rest a little."

Later that day, I spotted half a dozen crows picking at the burn pile when I went out to the shed to see Cotton. The charred bedding sat on the top of the mound like a big black turd dropped from a thundercloud. And bits of mattress ticking dotted the yard like black and white cotton bolls.

"Hey, Lucas." Cotton looked up at me as the crows scattered. "I hear y'all roasted some hot dogs out here yesterday and had a big party."

"We almost roasted Robert."

"That what Corinthia tol' me. She say you had to pull him outa the closet."

"Yeah, I guess he thought it was a safe place to hide."

"So you the big hero now." Cotton put down his wrench and leaned against the tractor.

"No one else was around." I shrugged, embarrassed. "I figured it'd be a lot better to pull him out than carry him out on a stretcher. You got a smoke?"

"Yep, gotta have 'em." Laughing, he wiped his hands on his pants and reached for the new pack of Camels in his pocket.

"After yesterday, I need a couple." I grabbed his pack as I looked over my shoulder.

"Hey, hey, take it easy. Robert all right, but what gonna happen to him when you not 'round?" he asked. "You can't tote him on your hip like a little kid or just stick him in a corner. He weigh more than the botha us and he gettin' bigger every day."

"I don't know—he's not my problem." I hated myself for thinking that way about my mother's baby brother, but I didn't want to get stuck taking care of Robert.

"He could be. When your grandparents pass, Alvin Earl won't wanna mess with him."

"All he wants to do is play cards and drink," I said, lighting a cigarette. "He'll likely send Robert to Maysville."

"Ohhh, I wouldn't send an ol' skunk to Maysville—too much bad stuff goin' on at that place."

"Corinthia already told me about the clogged toilets and patients running around naked."

"There stuff goin' on a whole lot worse than that."

I exhaled real slow and asked, "What kind of stuff are you talking about?"

"My friend Buford workin' in the laundry over there, but he go all over the grounds. He say those doctors puts the more violent-like folks in cages, and they does some kinda sterilization surgery on mens."

"Sterilization surgery?"

"Yeah, they cuts off their balls just like they cuts the balls off a horse."

"They geld them?" I winced and my hands went to my crotch.

"They castrates 'em. And Buford say he never hear anyone yell and scream like some poor man gettin' his balls cut off."

"Does anyone know patients are being sterilized and locked up in cages?"

"I don't know. Mosta the folks there ain't got no family, and if they does, the families forgets about 'em."

"Maybe the families are ashamed of them," I said.

"Maybe. Some folks ends up dyin' in that place from 'spicious circumstances."

"Suspicious circumstances—what does that mean?"

Cotton wrapped his hands around his throat. "Accordin' to Buford, it mean they been choked to death or beat with a club by onea the workers."

"God Almighty! Corinthia didn't tell me about that."

"She likely don't know. And she likely don't know a lota 'em don't get a tombstone."

"No tombstone? Everyone has a tombstone." I thought about the hours I'd spent scrubbing tombstones with Clorox and an old brush in our family cemetery.

"Mosta the folks there ain't got no money. When they dies, the workers just dumps 'em in graves out in some pasture."

"You can't just beat somebody to death and then dump their body out in a pasture. That's against the law."

"I ain't no lawyer—I just tellin' you what Buford done tol' me. One day he had to help dig the graves."

And you believe everything he told you?" I asked.

"He ain't got no reason to lie."

## 15

For the next week we aired out the house. Little George replaced the window frames and glass in our bedroom. Robert picked up loose nails and scraps of wood, and I scrubbed and helped paint the walls. Granny ordered a new mattress from the Sears in Macon and made us some new curtains.

While we waited for the mattress, Robert and I slept on the back porch. And every night he tried to count the fireflies as I listened to the crickets and frogs. During the day, he followed me around the farm like a clumsy shadow. He even sat with me at the kitchen table when I did my homework. He practiced writing our names with a big fat pencil like the kids used in first grade while I wrote an essay for English class.

We only had a few more weeks of school, and Amelia and I were supposed to work on a history project on the battle of Gettysburg. Despite all of Mr. Goodman's blackboard diagrams, I was a lot more interested in World War II than I was in the Civil War since Nathan T., Little George and Corinthia's son, was still missing in action. But Amelia was the smartest student in the class, and I was glad Mr. Goodman paired us up. She was different from the other girls in my grade and wasn't afraid to be different.

"Maybe we could work on the project after school," she whispered as we waited for the dismissal bell in history class. She hesitated a minute and asked, "Could you come home with me one day?"

"Uhhh, I don't know." I was surprised by her question. None of the girls had ever invited me to their house before, except for Emily Anne. She'd invited our Sunday school class over for a picnic back in the seventh grade. I'd brought one of Corinthia's coconut cream cakes, and after we ate we all played Bible charades, the most boring game ever invented. I couldn't wait to go home.

"I'll have to check with my grandmother. I live with her and my step-grandfather."

"Do you have a telephone?" she asked.

"Yeah, and we've got indoor plumbing."

Paw Paw hated the idea of speaking into a machine as much as he hated the idea of using a mechanical picker in the fields. But Granny insisted on getting a phone last year. She said she wanted to be able to call the doctor in case someone got sick.

"Oh, I'm sorry. I know a lot of the kids who live on farms don't have phones. Maybe you can call me or tell me at school tomorrow." She scribbled some numbers on a scrap of paper and dropped it on my desk as she headed out the door.

After supper that night, I told Granny I was working on a history project with a new girl. "She wants me to come by her house one day after school to work on some posters."

"Who's the girl?" she asked.

"Amelia Weinstein." I hoped she wouldn't ask me a lot of questions.

"Oh, Caroline's granddaughter. If Caroline's going to be there, you can go over next Friday. But someone will have to pick you up."

"When I get my scooter, I'll be able to ride back and forth to school on my own."

Granny ignored my comment about the scooter, but Corinthia said, "If Little George too busy, I comes and gets you. Everybody know where Miss Caroline live."

Even though I told Amelia I could come over on Friday, we didn't speak much during the week. And I wished I hadn't told her I'd come over. When Friday finally rolled around, I woke up feeling kind of nervous. I started to put on my pressed Sunday shirt, but decided I didn't want anyone to notice I was dressed up.

"Are you going to see your girlfriend?" asked Robert.

"Girlfriend—what are you talking about? I'm going to work on a project with Amelia."

"Lucas got a girlfriend. Lucas got a girlfriend." He teased as he watched me get dressed. "Are you going to kiss her?"

"I told you—we're working on a project. Now, get out of my way. I'm trying to get all my books together." I hurried to the kitchen.

"Mornin', Lucas." Corinthia put a bowl of grits on the table. "You ready for some eggs?"

"No, I got to go—and Robert better stay in here and have his breakfast." Picking up my project cardboard and a biscuit, I headed outside to wait for the bus.

I hadn't said anything to the other kids about going to Amelia's grandmother's house, and neither had Amelia. But somehow the word leaked out, and now the Overton boys had something else to harass me about besides Robert.

When they saw me with the cardboard, they hung out the bus window and George yelled, "Y'all going to draw some dirty pictures? Is that new girl going to take off her clothes for you?"

"Maybe you'll get to twist her little titty," said Carlton as I stepped on the bus.

"Or maybe she'll give you a little twist if you're lucky!" hooted George.

Their taunting made me mad. Except for giving Betty Jean, Alvin Earl's ex-wife, a polite peck on the check, I'd never kissed a girl or even put my arm around one. Not even on a dare. But I thought it might be nice to kiss Amelia even if she was skinny and flat-chested.

"Lucas, you better get out quick," said Carlton as we pulled into the school parking lot. "You don't want to keep that little Amelia waiting."

"Shut up!" I got off the bus and headed to the library. I stayed there until it was time for the last morning bell. Then I rushed to homeroom and slid into my seat without even a glance at Amelia.

"Hey," she whispered. "You're coming over today, right?"

"Just for a little while." I kept my eyes on the notebook on my desk and didn't say another word to her for the rest of the day.

After the final bell rang, I stopped by the school library again and took my time getting back to my locker. I waited until the halls were clear. I didn't want any of the kids to see me walking out of the building with Amelia.

She was waiting by my locker with an armload of books when I finally walked up. "I thought you forgot," she said softly.

"Oh, no. I had to return an overdue book to the library." I was surprised by how easily I could lie and how quickly she believed me.

By the time we left the building, the schoolyard was quiet. "Let me take your books," I said, barely glancing at her. My voice sounded strange, and I realized this was the first time I'd been alone with her. I grabbed her books, and when my hand accidentally brushed up against her sleeve, my cheeks got hot.

"Thank you, Lucas," she said in a stiff voice.

We didn't say much as we walked a few blocks to her grandmother's house, a big two-story white home with fat columns and a wide porch surrounded by neatly trimmed hedges. Granny told me the house had been built before the Civil War by slaves and was one of the oldest homes in the state. I'd walked by it a million times but had never been inside.

"Hello, Lucas," Amelia's grandmother called from the porch. She was tall and thin, with a long string of pearls draped around her neck and sparkly rings on both hands. As soon as I saw her, I felt certain she didn't wear nightgowns made out of old seed sacks like Granny did.

"How are your grandmother and Robert doing?" she asked. "I heard there was a fire at the farm."

"Yes, ma'am," I said. "We had a little fire in the bedroom, but everyone is fine."

"I need to get out to see her," she said. "Y'all can work on the porch where it's nice and cool. I'll bring out some cookies and tea."

Miss Caroline brought out a silver tray with tea glasses—not Mason jars—and a plate of store-bought cookies. Amelia spread out our materials on an old wicker table, and we sipped tea with strange-looking green leaves floating on the top. I tried to fish them out with my finger when Amelia wasn't looking, but she knew what I was doing and said, "My grandmother always uses mint as a garnish."

I never heard of garnish. I didn't want to sound stupid, but I wasn't sure what to do with the leaves. "Do you eat them?"

"No, no, they're just for decoration." Giving me a slight smile, she picked up a silver spoon and scooped them out. "Not even rabbits would eat those leaves."

"That's a relief." I laughed, wiping my fingers on my pants. And then, for the first time since I'd met Amelia, she laughed too, in a real, girly way.

She glanced at the cardboard resting on the table. "I can draw a map of one of the battlefields."

"I think you could draw about anything," I said, wondering if I should tell her that her sketch of Lassie got burned up in the fire.

"Thanks, Lucas. Maybe you can do something about some of the generals—Mr. Goodman would love that."

"Sure. I can't draw, but I can write a report and read it. And maybe I can tell some jokes like Mr. Goodman."

"I hope your jokes will be funnier than his."

"Anybody's jokes would be funnier than Mr. Goodman's." I peered through the door into the deep front hall with polished hardwood floors. I spotted a central staircase and a lot of old pictures hanging on the walls. "Living in a big house must be kind of creepy."

"Most of the time it's just kind of quiet and lonely," Amelia said. "I don't even know most of the people in those portraits."

"My grandmother has a lot of old pictures, too." Then I added, "I guess it must be hard coming to a new school in the middle of the year."

She nodded. "I had a lot of friends at my old school— nobody ever said anything about the way I talked or my father being Jewish. But I think I'll be going back to New York with my mother. She doesn't want to be stuck in a small town with nothing to do."

I didn't like to think of Amelia moving back to New York, but I said, "I know what you mean. Have you ever seen Niagara Falls?"

"My dad took us a couple of years ago. We got special raincoats and boots and actually went to a cave under the falls. It was really noisy and we got soaked, but it was fun."

"You've been to Canada?"

"Only to see the falls."

"Sounds like you've done some traveling."

"We used to go to Atlantic City almost every summer. But my dad started a new job and says he doesn't have time to go to the beach."

"I want to see Niagara Falls and the ocean—I've never been to a beach."

"I love to walk in the sand early in the morning when it's quiet. You can smell the salt water and look for shells."

"You ever been fishing in the ocean?"

"No." She wrinkled up her nose and started sketching a map on the big cardboard. "Nobody in my family fishes."

"Your family doesn't know what they're missing," I said as if I were an expert on outdoor activities. "I used to fish all the time in our pond with J.T., the boy who used to sit in your desk."

"You've got a pond on your farm?" She sounded amazed.

"Yeah, and we've got a creek, too. Corinthia, our cook, says the pond's more like a big puddle than a pond, but it's got a lot of fish and some turtles."

"I don't know if I could stick a worm on a hook."

"That's just like Robert."

"Robert?"

"My uncle. He's my mother's younger brother and he lives on the farm."

"Oh, right. My grandmother told me about him."

"I help him bait his hooks." I wondered what her grandmother had said about Robert and what she'd heard from the other kids. But for some reason, I kept on talking. "I could help you bait your hooks. And maybe we could go fishing sometime," I said, hardly believing the words pouring out of my mouth.

"Do you promise to put the worm on the hook, Lucas?"

"Cross my heart."

16

The first thing Cotton said to me when I saw him the next morning was something about my project. "I hear you workin' real hard with your girlfriend. What's her name?"

"Amelia."

"She the girl from New York—right? I done some yard work for her grandmomma. But she real particular 'bout her bushes. You gots to trim 'em just so."

"Yeah, but she ain't my girlfriend."

"That not what Robert sayin'."

"He's just talking to hear himself talk. I ain't got time for girlfriends."

"You ain't got the money either." His eyes dancing, he rolled his hips. "They expensive and they always wantin' something new and pretty."

"I ain't had as much experience as you. You're the ladies' man, but just give me some time to catch up."

"Well, you ain't gonna get any time. We gotta start hoein' and choppin' that cotton. Mr. Harold up to gettin' out in the fields today?"

"I don't know. He's still in the bed."

"He don't look real good."

Paw Paw took lots of medicine for his heart and rested in the afternoons. Even though Corinthia cooked liver and fresh vegetables for him, he was losing weight. She tried to coax him into eating, but he didn't have much of an appetite. His color was bad and he could barely walk to the kitchen. He spent more and more of his time sitting in a chair in the old parlor staring out at the fields.

One afternoon when he got up to go to the bathroom after his nap, we heard a loud thud. We rushed into the parlor and found him crumpled on the floor next to the piano. He was conscious, but he had a big, red gash on his hand.

"You all right, Paw Paw?" I asked.

"What happened, Harold?" Granny asked, kneeling down next to him. "Are you all right?"

"I started feeling kind of dizzy and lost my balance. I tried to catch myself and hit my hand against the piano," Paw Paw said, sounding weak.

"Just be still, Mr. Harold, and we get you up," Corinthia said. "Lucas, Cotton already gone home, but Little George out in the barn. Go get him."

"Did Daddy get cut?" asked Robert, staring at Paw Paw's hand.

"I think he's going to be all right," said Granny. She sounded calm, but I could tell she didn't want to scare Robert.

"I gets a towel with some cool water and a little turpentine for his hand," said Corinthia.

I ran out to the barn and found Little George fixing a bridle. As soon as I told him Paw Paw fell, he dropped the bridle and hurried toward the house. "Miz Lettie, where Mr. Harold? He hurtin' bad?" he called out as he flung open the screen door.

"We're in here," Granny said, pressing a cool cloth to Paw Paw's hand. "He just took a little spill and now we want to get him into bed."

"Mr. Harold, you all right?" asked Little George.

"You needs to call somebody if you gotta get up," Corinthia said.

"I just got a little dizzy," Paw Paw said. "I'll be all right."

Little George got on one side of Paw Paw and I got on his other side. We propped him up and slowly walked to his bedroom. "You just takes it real easy now. We gots you," Little George said.

Granny and Corinthia plumped up the pillows and we eased him down on the bed. Little George and I lifted his legs and Granny took off his shoes.

"Harold, I'm going to call Dr. Trent. Little George and the boys will sit with you. Lucas, cover him up with the quilt," Granny said.

"No, it's too hot for that quilt," Paw Paw said. "Corinthia, how about getting me some tea? Take Robert with you and let Lucas pull the shades down. I want to talk with Little George a minute."

"You feelin' better, Mr. Harold?" asked Little George.

I took my time adjusting the shades. I wanted to hear what Paw Paw had to say to Little George.

"Yes, I'm a little better," Paw Paw said, leaning against the pillows. "But there's not much the doctor can do for me now."

"You just gots to rest some and start eatin' more," Little George said.

"We all got to die sometime, and my heart's about wore out. When I pass, Alvin Earl will get the farm—my grandpa bought this land and I want it to stay in my family."

"I understands." Little George nodded and I fiddled with the curtains.

Paw Paw dropped his voice and I struggled to hear. "Alvin Earl doesn't care about farming—his momma ruined him when they moved into Crisscross. She'd never let him get his hands dirty or play outside with other kids. He'd just as soon sell this place to get the cash. But he's still my son."

"You needs to rest some, Mr. Harold." Little George moved toward the door.

"Let me finish." Paw Paw seemed to forget I was in the room and went on. "My will says Alvin Earl must care for Miss Lettie and the boys, especially Robert. And he must let you and Corinthia stay on. Your family's been on this farm almost as long as we've been farming."

"You always been good to my folks and me. I be crippled up real bad if you hadn't took me to that white doctor when I fell outa that tree."

"I know you'll help Miss Lettie. And maybe Cotton will stay on, too. He likes to sneak a smoke now and then, but he's a good worker."

"No one ever know what Cotton gonna do. But Corinthia and me do all we can. You best gets some rest now."

79

Paw Paw closed his eyes. Then, suddenly opening them, he called out. "Wait. If anything happens to Alvin Earl and Miss Lettie, the farm will go to Lucas. And he'll need your help, too."

Surprised to hear I was next in line for the farm, I looked at Paw Paw and then at Little George. But he backed away from Paw Paw's bed and motioned for me to follow.

"I help him all I can," Little George said.

"And don't let Alvin Earl send Robert off to that state hospital." Paw Paw closed his eyes again and let out a tired sigh.

"I 'spect loosin' another chil' just 'bout break Miz Lettie's heart. I knows it just 'bout broke mine."

As we left the room, I saw tears in Little George's eyes. And I knew he was thinking about Nathan T.

## 17

Dr. Trent came to see Paw Paw every other day, but he never got over his fall. He spent the next couple of weeks in bed. His face was drawn and tight looking, and his pajama top hung off his bony shoulders like a shirt flapping on the backyard line.

Granny sat by his bedside, talking with him about the farm and sponging him off with a cool towel. Sometimes I read the *Crisscross Crier* to him, even though I hated to go in the sickroom where the blinds were always halfway drawn and everything smelled like Clorox. But Paw Paw usually dozed off by the time I finished reading the first page.

One Sunday afternoon when Paw Paw was feeling a little better, Alvin Earl came by the house. Granny had called him to tell him his daddy wanted to speak with him. After he went into the sickroom, I brought them both some iced tea.

Then I sat outside on the front porch so I could hear them talking through the window. I was glad Corinthia wasn't around to fuss at me about killing the cat with curiosity.

"What's on your mind, Daddy?" Alvin Earl asked. I could hear the familiar metal clicking of his lighter as he flicked it open and closed.

"I want you to settle down," Paw Paw said. "Quit drinking and playing cards with that crowd in Crisscross or wherever it is you go. Take care of the farm."

"It always comes down to the cards and the drinking, don't it?" His voice had a hard edge to it.

"After you went to that hospital up in Atlanta, you promised you'd settle down and raise a family."

"I didn't say anything about having kids. Betty Jean was the one who wanted to have a bunch of kids—not me."

"Having kids is your business—just find a nice girl and treat her good."

"What about Miss Lettie and Robert?"

"Let them have the old house. You can save up and build yourself a new place. You can build it as big as you want."

"And what about Lucas? He's got more sense than Robert, but not a whole lot more."

I listened more carefully when I heard my name, even though I didn't like Alvin Earl comparing me to Robert.

"Lucas's going to be graduating from high school soon. He won't be around much longer. But Little George will likely stay on to help out."

"You're always thinking about that gimpy nigger!" flared Alvin Earl.

"You need to work with him, Alvin Earl," said Paw Paw. "He'll help you bring in a crop."

"How come you're always taking up for Little George? A nigger's a nigger, Daddy."

"Little George ain't your ordinary nigger. He's got some white blood in him."

"So do half the niggers in South Georgia. White blood don't make them special—it just makes them a little smarter."

"He's a lot smarter and he knows every inch of this farm. He'll get you a good price at the gin." Paw Paw coughed a couple of times and tried to clear his throat. "Just promise me you'll look for a nice girl and try to work with Little George."

"I'll look for a girl. You know I've never had any problems getting women, colored or white." Alvin Earl chuckled in a mean way. "But I can't give you any promise about Little George. He needs to move on."

"Go on now," Paw Paw said, struggling to get a breath. "I'm worn out and can't argue with you. You're going to do what you want to do—you always do."

"That's right, Daddy—I've got to look out for myself." Without another word, he headed out.

Later that afternoon, after Paw Paw had rested some, Granny went into the sick room to talk with him about his will. They kept their voices down, but I heard Paw Paw say something about a letter for Little George. I wasn't sure what they were talking about. But I figured it had something to do with the farm when Granny said she'd call Mr. Barnett, Paw Paw's lawyer.

The next day, Mr. Barnett, a small, slight man with a deep voice who sang in the church choir, drove out to the house. When I opened the door to let him in, he had a pair of crooked glasses perched on his nose and wore a wrinkled suit that looked like it had been rolled up on his back seat for three weeks. He had a black briefcase stuffed with papers under his arm.

"Good to see you, Lucas," he said, offering me his hand. "How's your grandpaw doing today? I've known him a long time and hope he'll be feeling better."

"Granny's with him now. She said to tell you to have a seat," I said, pointing to the couch. "She'll be out in a minute."

"I apologize for the last-minute call, David," said Granny when she came into the parlor. "Harold insists on making these changes, but I may have to help him hold the pen."

"No problem, Lettie, as long as he's clear-headed and knows what he wants," Mr. Barnett said. "I've drawn up the papers. We need to get a neighbor to serve as a witness."

Granny hesitated. "You know the Ledbetters have moved and the postman has already come by today."

"I can go get Little George," I said. "He's out in the shed."

"No, no." Mr. Barnett cleaned his glasses with the tip of his tie and shuffled through a thick folder. "The witness can't be anyone connected to the family."

"Little George has worked here a long time, but he's not kin," I said.

Glancing at Granny, Mr. Barnett said, "It would be better if I called someone from my office to come out."

"Whatever you think, David," said Granny. "Let me show you where the telephone is."

18

A few days after Mr. Barnett's visit, Paw Paw stopped speaking and drifted in and out. He slept all the time and barely opened his eyes when Granny said his name. His cheeks were sunken in, and he was so thin he almost disappeared between the sheets.

"Paw Paw looks real bad," I said to Corintha. "Is he going to just sleep away?"

"It won't be long now—his breathing real shallow-like," she said, carrying soiled sheets out of the sickroom. "I prays he have an easy passin'. Your grandmomma 'bout wore out and I is, too."

Granny stayed in the sickroom for the next three days. She wouldn't leave Paw Paw's side. Reverend Morris came to the house late one night to sit with her and read verses from his Bible. And right after Reverend Morris left, Paw Paw died while Granny dozed by his bedside.

I was just about asleep when she came into the bedroom and stood by Robert's bed. She'd been crying, but she was calm. "Boys, Paw Paw's gone now and out of pain."

"Daddy's gone?" asked Robert, rubbing his eyes.

Granny gripped his hand. "Yes, he's leaving this earth and all its suffering."

"Where's Daddy now?" asked Robert.

"He's still in the bedroom. You can see him tomorrow."

I pulled back the covers and swung my feet over the side of the bed, but Granny touched my shoulder. "I've already called Dr. Trent and the funeral home. And I'll call Alvin Earl and Cousin William."

"What do you want me to do, Granny?"

"There's nothing you can do, Lucas, but wait until tomorrow. After Mr. Duncan brings him back from the funeral home, we'll lay him out in the parlor. I want him here with the family before the burial."

Relieved that I didn't have to go into the sickroom, I said, "I'll stay with Robert."

"Good. I'm going to sit with Paw Paw until they come. Y'all go back to sleep." Granny quietly slipped out.

I stretched out again and thought about my step-grandfather. I'd always spent more time with Little George than I did with Paw Paw when I was a little kid. Little George used to hold me on his lap when he drove the tractor, and he taught me how to bait a hook. Paw Paw never said much, but I knew he was there if Robert or I ever really needed him. Trying to imagine what life on the farm would be like without him, I tossed and turned until I finally fell asleep.

Before dawn, I woke up, panting and soaked in sweat. I had the same nightmare I'd had right after J.T.'s daddy committed suicide. But this time I wasn't by myself. I was standing on a cliff with Robert. I told him not to get too close to the edge, but he wanted to see the valley below. When I yelled at him and tried to grab his arm, he shook me off and stumbled on a rock. I reached for his arm and hollered his name as he disappeared over the edge. I ran to the edge of the cliff and watched him tumble into a dark ravine. I woke up before he hit the bottom, but I wondered if anyone heard me screaming *Robert, Robert!*

Folks say bad news travels fast, but in Crisscross it travels like the speed of light. Robert and I were still having breakfast the next morning when neighbors started coming by with covered dishes and food. After we finished our grits, Little George and I moved the couch and the marble-topped table. Robert carried the family Bible with the tooled leather cover and put it on the table.

As we pushed the couch against the wall, Granny came into the parlor and opened the Bible to the very beginning, the section with the family record. Carefully turning to the "Deaths" page, she picked up a fountain pen and, without saying a word, added Paw Paw's name right under my mother and daddy's names. Then she went into the kitchen for a minute and came back with a bunch of pink and red roses from her garden. She closed the Bible and put the flowers on the marble-topped table.

When Mr. Duncan, the Crisscross undertaker, and his assistants arrived with Paw Paw's body, the house was filled with the sweet smell of Granny's blooms. Robert and I stood beside the table while the undertaker's assistants placed Paw Paw's casket on the folding stand and put it in front of the parlor windows. Robert moved closer to me as Mr. Duncan slowly opened the lid. He straightened the light blue quilt draped over Paw Paw's legs and the white ribbon that said "Beloved Husband and Father" in gold letters.

"They put Daddy in that big box?" asked Robert.

Granny closed her eyes and nodded. "He's just resting there for a while."

Pointing to the coffin, Robert said, "That's not my daddy."

"Oh, he your daddy," said Little George in a gentle voice. "They just cleaned him up real good and he ain't wearin' his hat."

I took a quick look at Paw Paw and thought about J.T.'s daddy, Mr. Ledbetter. I wondered if the funeral director had gotten him all cleaned up after he jumped off that bridge near the county line. I got chill bumps when I thought about what he must have looked like when Sheriff Norton found him in the creek bed. And I remembered Paw Paw saying no one in their right mind would want to look at someone who'd jumped off a thirty-foot bridge.

After Mr. Duncan and his assistants left, Robert and I took a couple of steps toward the coffin. But Robert was right—the man stretched out on the satiny material with his hands folded together in prayer didn't look at all like Paw Paw. He looked like one of those dummies in Bailey's Department Store window in Crisscross. Except that his eyes were closed. His hair was plastered to his head and his face was so smooth and shiny that it looked like it was coated with wax. I'd never seen him wear a tie while he was alive, but he was dressed in a starched white shirt with a polka-dotted bow-tie and his best pair of overalls.

"He wanted to be buried in his bib overalls," said Granny, leaning over the coffin. "He said nobody would recognize him if he was laid out in a fancy suit."

"Well, he look real peaceful, Miz Lettie," said Little George, tears spilling down his cheeks. "And I don't think St. Peter care what he be wearin'."

It almost hurt me more to see Little George quietly crying than it did to see Paw Paw lying in his polished coffin. The only other time I'd seen him cry was when he heard that Nathan T. was missing.

"Sometimes it seems like all we do on this earth is weep and grieve, but I think he was ready to go," said Granny softly. "Burying a man who's almost seventy-five is not like burying a baby or a young person."

"That true. When all those boys die in the war, you feels like they been cheated. It just don't seem fair," said Little George. And I knew he was thinking about his own missing son.

Granny reached in the coffin and adjusted Paw Paw's glasses and straightened his tie as if he were going to stand up and greet folks at the front door. She didn't mind touching him. I'd seen lots of dead animals covered with maggots and went to the funeral for Mr. Terrell, our postman. But even when J.T. double-dog dared me to touch Mr. Terrell's hand, I didn't want to get too close. And I didn't want to get too close to PawPaw.

I didn't like having his body in the house overnight. I didn't want to remember him lying in a big box wearing a starched shirt or struggling to get a breath in the sickroom. Just like I wanted to remember J.T.'s daddy sitting on the porch laughing and joking while we were playing ball, I wanted to remember Paw Paw gazing out on the fields, sweating and sunburned while he mopped his face with his old felt hat.

"Is Daddy going to heaven with the angels?" asked Robert.

"Not yet," said Granny, pushing a strand of hair off her forehead. "Some friends and neighbors want to come by the house to tell him goodbye first."

"Tell him goodbye?" asked Robert in a puzzled voice. "Can he hear them talking?"

"He knows they're coming just like he knows we're here now," said Granny.

"When is he going to heaven?" Robert asked. "He doesn't have his hat."

"He doesn't need his hat now. He'll go to heaven after the service tomorrow," I said, trying to help him understand that going to heaven wasn't like taking a road trip to Atlanta. "After all the neighbors come and the preacher says a special prayer, he'll go to heaven with his hat."

"Is he coming back?" asked Robert.

"No, he won't come back. But he'll be with God and all the angels. It'll be real nice. He'll see Lizba, my mother—your sister—and my daddy," I said.

"Can I go with him?" Robert screwed up his face and looked hopeful. "I want to see Lizba and Clementine."

"Clementine?" I didn't know what to say—I'd forgotten about burying one of Robert's hens near Granny's rose garden.

"You're not going anywhere for a long time, Robert," said Granny, giving him a hug. "I couldn't get along without you."

Robert didn't say anything else, and I knew he didn't understand about being in heaven with God. But neither did I.

## 19

Paw Paw said funerals were for the living. While he was still thinking straight, he told Granny to just stick him in the ground after he died. He didn't want a long, drawn-out service and some preacher he barely knew telling everyone what a fine man he was. And he didn't want folks he hadn't seen in ten years gobbling up Corinthia's fried chicken and leaving dirty dishes all over the place.

But if the weather was sunny and clear, even a graveside service was a major event in Crisscross. And Paw Paw and Granny knew just about everyone in the county. Mr. Duncan and his assistants came out early the next morning to prepare for the crowd. Cordelle, Cotton's high school friend, dug the grave, and the assistants put up a tent with the words *We Provide Unsurpassed Service* embroidered on the flap over the burial site. They placed a dark blue rug under the tent with *Duncan's* stamped on it. Then they set up a row of folding chairs for the family on the rug and more rows of chairs outside the tent.

The sun was almost directly overhead as we stood in the yard greeting folks. Sheriff Norton and Deputy Kelly, dressed in freshly pressed uniforms, were among the first to arrive. Nodding to Granny, the sheriff said, "Miss Lettie, I'm real sorry about Mr. Harold. I've known him all my life. I remember seeing him at the feed store when I was just a boy."

"I'm glad we can bury him in the family plot," said Granny. "I appreciate y'all being here today and so would he."

"Well," he said, "I wanted to pay my respects." He tipped his hat and headed toward the cemetery.

As he walked off, Mr. Duncan came up to us and said, "It's about time to begin. Y'all go ahead and take your seats in the tent."

Granny checked her watch and scanned the yard and gravel lot. "Where's Alvin Earl? We all need to sit together."

"He can't even get here on time for his own daddy's service," I said under my breath. "He's probably at Gordy's."

"Look, here he comes. Don't say anything to set him off," she said. "And stay with Robert."

"Yes, ma'am." I held on to Robert's arm. "Stand by me and don't be picking at that mole on your elbow."

"Alvin Earl," Granny called, motioning for him to hurry. "Reverend Morris is about ready to start. Come walk with us."

Alvin Earl got out of his truck and strode toward us in a rumpled suit. Even though he'd shaved, his face looked bloated. He grunted something to a neighbor, but he didn't say much to us. And he walked by himself as we headed to the graveside tent.

Almost every chair was filled, and I saw Little George and Cotton standing off by themselves at a respectful distance. They were dressed up in white shirts, and it was the first time I'd seen Cotton without his cap and glove. He gave me a slight wave and small smile. And I wished he and Little George were sitting next to Robert and me under the tent instead of Alvin Earl.

While Reverend Morris droned on about our brother Harold, I stared at Paw Paw's coffin. I could smell the freshly turned soil along the edge of his grave, and I heard folks sniffling behind me. I tried to focus on what Reverend Morris was saying. But I kept wondering what it would feel like to be stretched out in a wooden box wearing a starched shirt and my best overalls.

I thought about what my parents' funeral must have been like almost thirteen years before. I didn't remember anything about their service. But I felt a rush of sadness when I realized I would never know them, and they would never know me. I realized Little George was right when he said it didn't seem fair when folks died young.

As Reverend Morris said the Twenty-third Psalm, Cordelle and Mr. Duncan's assistants began to lower the casket into the deep hole with thick ropes. Robert whispered to me in a loud voice, "What are they doing?"

"They're getting ready for Paw Paw to go to heaven."

"What's heaven?" he asked me for the hundredth time since yesterday.

"Remember we talked about heaven and being with God."

"When's he going?" he continued. "Does he have his hat?"

"Soon. The angels are waiting for him."

"Where's the angels now?" Turning in his chair, he craned his neck to look for the angels in the crowd. "I don't see them."

As I pointed toward the sky, Alvin Earl tapped me on the shoulder and said, "Shut him up."

I nodded and whispered to Robert, "Shhh! The preacher's getting ready to say a prayer."

Reverend Morris dropped a handful of clay on Paw Paw's coffin and said some closing words. A few folks in the crowd echoed "Amen," and Mr. Duncan magically appeared next to Granny. He touched her elbow and gave her the carefully folded ribbon with the gold letters saying "Beloved Father and Husband" that had been in Paw Paw's casket.

When the service was finally over, folks rushed up to speak with us. Neighbors pumped my hand and patted me on the back, telling me how sorry they were about Paw Paw and how big I'd gotten. Some said I favored my mother, and others said I favored my father. Miss Gilbert, my homeroom teacher, pulled me toward her and gave me a big hug. My cheeks ached from the smile stuck on my face.

After a few minutes, Alvin Earl headed toward three men waiting in the gravel lot by his truck. I didn't recognize the men, but they all seemed to know each other. They lit up cigarettes, talking and laughing like they were ready to play a game of horseshoes. Two were dressed in white shirts with rolled-up sleeves and dark trousers. One of them wore a crumpled fedora and had stubble on his cheeks. The third one had a thick red face and wore a cowboy hat and faded blue jeans.

As they were talking, the cowboy pushed back the rim of his hat. He slapped Alvin Earl on the back. And then with a quick, jerky movement he took a pint of whiskey out of his hip pocket. Looking to the left and the right, he said, "Try some of this, boys. It's factory-made and guaranteed to sharpen your pencil." The men hooted as he took a swig and passed the pint around the group.

After the bottle went all the way around the little circle, Alvin Earl took an extra swig and said, "Just what I needed." He wiped his mouth with the back of his hand and passed the bottle back to the cowboy.

Corinthia stood on the back porch, scowling at Alvin Earl and the men gathered around him. "Ain't they got no respect for the dead?"

"I think they're from Gordy's," I said.

"I knows where they's from—you don't needs to tell me. They ain't got no business bein' here today. You go on in the house and check on Robert."

The Co'Cola thermometer on the back porch read 92 degrees. Granny had two small fans—one in the dining room and one in the parlor—blowing air around, but it was still hot and stuffy. The house was packed. And I was wearing my wool suit with the itchy, too-short pants.

Most folks were gathered around the dining room table to fill their plates. The men had stripped off their coats and loosened their ties while they talked about a possible drought and the price of cotton. The women waved funeral home fans in the air as they traded recipes. I wasn't very hungry, but Robert stood by the table stuffing coconut cake and pecan pie in his mouth like he hadn't eaten in a week. He wiped his nose on his shirtsleeve and then reached for more pie.

"Use your handkerchief," whispered Corinthia. She wore her best white apron and picked up dirty plates as fast as folks put them down. Turning toward me, she said, "If your Paw Paw seed all these folks snatchin' up my chicken like a pack of hungry wolves, he be sayin' I done told y'all. And he ain't even cold." She hurried into the kitchen to get more clean glasses.

I nodded and caught sight of Emily Anne Morris, the preacher's daughter, out of the corner of my eye. Granny and most of the other women wore black, but she had on a fluffy bubblegum-pink dress and pranced around like a pony in a show ring. I wanted to run out to the shed where Cotton was sitting or walk in the backwoods where it was cool and quiet. But I knew Granny expected me to speak to Emily Anne.

"I'm sorry about your grandpa," she said, flicking her hair back. "My mother told me he got real sick toward the end." She smoothed out her dress, and I noticed that her fingernails were bubblegum pink, too.

"Thanks." I didn't feel like talking about Paw Paw with Emily Anne or anyone else. His death felt too close.

"My mother bought this dress in Atlanta and this is the first time I've worn it." She twirled around and I caught a whiff of some kind of perfume that made me want to sneeze.

"Oh." I wasn't sure what I was supposed to say.

"I'm the only girl at school who wears store-bought clothes. I never wear anything homemade."

I didn't know anything about girls' clothes, but I thought about the plaid jumpers Amelia wore. Digging my hands in my pockets, I wished I was talking to Amelia instead of Emily Anne. Her grandmother had called Granny yesterday and said they were going to Atlanta for a few days to see Amelia's mother. But somehow I knew if Amelia were here, she wouldn't be telling me about her fancy dresses.

When Emily Anne spotted Robert standing by the table gorging himself on desserts, she studied him as if he was some kind of specimen from science class. "Does he ever say anything?"

"Sure, but sometimes he's hard to understand."

"Every time I see him, he's eating something and picking his nose. My aunt says he should be in the state hospital."

"Who?"

"My Aunt Rosemary—she's a nurse and she says he should be in the Maysville hospital where he can get proper care."

"Proper care? Does she know Robert?"

"She's seen him around Crisscross."

"I need to go help Corinthia." I picked up a couple of dirty glasses and turned toward the kitchen. I wasn't going to listen to Emily Ann or anyone else tell me how to take care of Robert.

Emily Anne stomped off and Corinthia whispered, "She talkin' to you 'bout her aunt?"

Nodding, I put the glasses on the sink.

"Her aunt think she real smart. She could run her mouth 'til Jesus come home. But she don't know nothin'."

"She should mind her own business."

"Just forget 'bout that Emily Anne and her aunt," said Corinthia. "Put this chicken out on the table and keep your eye on Robert. He still eatin'."

When I headed back into the dining room, I saw Betty Jean coming toward me. It was the first time I'd seen her since she'd left Alvin Earl, and I was glad she still had her dimples. After I set the platter down on the table, she hugged me, her breasts pressing against my chest. I could feel myself getting hard. I quickly stepped back, afraid she might notice.

"How are you boys doing?" she asked, flashing me a big smile.

"Daddy's gone to heaven," said Robert in a way that sounded like he still thought Paw Paw was going to Atlanta for the day. Bits of pecan and coconut dotted the front of his shirt, and his glasses were smudged with frosting.

"That's right." Nodding, Betty Jean looked at me to make sure she'd understood what Robert had said. "He's with the angels now."

"I'm going to heaven, too," said Robert.

"I hope we all are. But not for a long time," I reminded him.

"Y'all are so tall and handsome," said Betty Jean. "Was that your girlfriend in the pink dress, Lucas?"

"Heck, no," I said. "That was Emily Anne Morris, the preacher's daughter."

"Now I remember her."

I could tell by the way Betty Jean said *her* that she didn't think much of Emily Anne either.

"Are you having a good year at school?" she asked. "I hear Miss Caroline's granddaughter is in your class."

"Her name is Amelia." My face felt warm as soon as I said her name. "She's from New York."

"That's what Miss Caroline told me. Sometimes she comes into my beauty shop. I hope her granddaughter is making some friends in Crisscross."

"Some of the kids say she's a Yankee because of the way she talks. But I think she's an artist." Before I could say anything about the sketch of the collie Amelia had drawn, Robert butted in.

"I got a girlfriend," he said.

"Did you say you have a girlfriend?" Betty Jean asked.

Robert's head bobbed up and down, and a smile spread across his face.

"Who's your girlfriend, Robert?" I wondered how Robert could have a girlfriend when he hardly ever left the farm.

"Betty Jean!" He slid his arm around her waist and rested his head on her shoulder.

"I'm flattered," she said in a surprised voice. "But you know I have someone I'm seeing in Albany, and I don't think I can manage two boyfriends."

"You have a boyfriend?" Robert looked like he was going to cry.

"Yes, and he's the jealous type. He wouldn't like it if he found out I had a boyfriend in Crisscross."

"I guess you're going to have to find another girlfriend, Robert," I said.

"While y'all are talking about your girlfriends," said Betty Jean with a quick wink, "I want to speak to Miss Lettie and

Corinthia." After nodding at Corinthia, she hugged Granny and said, "I'm so sorry about Mr. Harold, Miss Lettie. I wish I'd gotten over here to see him before he got so sick."

"He pretty much stopped eating and speaking the last few days before he died. But he always liked you, and we were all real sad when things didn't work out with you and Alvin Earl."

"I was, too, but I'm getting on with my life," Betty Jean said.

"I heard you've got a fellow in Albany, but we still miss you," said Granny, brushing by me to greet more of the neighbors. "Come back and see us."

"Just try and come sometime when Alvin Earl ain't around," I whispered.

20

After the funeral service, Granny put Paw Paw's beat-up field hat on her bedside table and shuffled around the house in her slippers. She played lots of hymns on the piano, and every afternoon she went into her bedroom to thumb through old photo albums. Every evening she went to the cemetery to sit by his grave with her Bible. When I tried to tell her about something that happened at school, she'd get kind of an empty look in her eyes and say in a faraway voice, "That's nice." And I knew she wasn't really listening.

"Granny's barely been out of the house since they buried Paw Paw," I said to Corinthia one morning in the kitchen. "She hasn't been out in her garden or gone to church."

"Your grandmomma and Mr. Harold married for almost thirty years," she said, scrubbing the breakfast skillet. "She need some time to grieve."

"Is she going to spend the rest of her life looking through old pictures and going to the cemetery?"

"I don't knows what she gonna do." Corinthia stopped scrubbing and stared out into the yard. "But I do knows most folks carry some grief if they lives long enough—you can't just pick it up and put it down like a hot pan. Sometimes it weigh you down so bad, it real hard to get outa bed in the mornin'."

I knew Corinthia was thinking about Nathan T. and said, "I miss Paw Paw, too, but I don't hang around the cemetery every day. And I bet J.T. ain't hanging around the cemetery either."

"He probably still too mad with his daddy for leavin' 'em the way he did to do much grievin'. That boy never got a chance to say goodbye and neither did his momma or sister."

"Granny's not mad at Paw Paw for dying and leaving her."

"Your Paw Paw live a full life and he ol' and sick. But J.T.'s daddy still have a lota good years. Maybe if y'all puts some geraniums on Mr. Harold's grave, that bring her some comfort."

The next morning, Robert and I carried watering cans to the cemetery and helped Granny plant the geraniums. "Your Paw Paw never liked flowers as much as I did," she said more to herself than to me. "But it's nice to have a bit of color by his grave."

"He always liked keeping the grass trimmed," I said.

"Yes, he did, Lucas. And it's going to be real different around here with just you and me and Robert now."

"As long as we've got Little George, we can manage."

"I hope so," said Granny with a worried look.

But she perked up later that afternoon when she got a typed letter from her cousin William in Columbia. He had an insurance meeting in Macon at the end of the week. And he wanted to drive to Crisscross to visit us since he and his wife Dorothy weren't able to come to the funeral.

A few days later, Cousin William drove up to the house in a new Chevy Sedan with a rocket-like silver hood ornament and whitewalls. He wore thick glasses and had pasty white skin that looked like it would turn blood red if he spent five minutes in the sun. He was dressed in a starched shirt with a matching tie and carried a big yellow box of Whitman's candy.

Granny rushed out to the yard to meet him as Robert and I trailed behind. "William, it's so good to see you. You remember the boys."

Giving Robert and me a quick nod, he hugged Granny and said, "Dorothy and I were so sorry to hear about Harold's passing. We wish we could have been here for the service, but I had to be in Charlotte for a meeting. I've been promoted and I'm doing a lot of traveling now."

"Well, come on in the house and we'll catch up," Granny said.

I'd never met Dorothy and could barely remember Cousin William, but he winked at me and pumped my hand like a man hoping to become the next mayor of Crisscross. "Lucas, you're looking more and more like your mother. I'm sure you have a lot of girlfriends," he said as he followed Granny up the front steps.

"No, not really," I stammered. His hand felt as soft as a woman's and his nails were buffed a pearly white. He wore a gold ring with a diamond the size of a nail head on his right little finger.

Cousin William grabbed Robert's hand and gave him the candy. "I know how much you love chocolate."

"Thank you," mumbled Robert, tearing at the wrapping.

Granny reached for the box and put it on the marble-topped table next to her Bible. "We'll just leave it here until we finish lunch. We don't want to spoil our appetites."

"Doesn't look like you eat much candy, Lucas," said Cousin William.

"I do, but I work it off," I said. "There's always lots to do around here."

"Well, everything looks about the same." William surveyed the parlor and Granny's photographs. "You've still got the big Bible and the old piano."

"I could never part with the piano." Opening the keyboard cover, Granny played a few chords. "You know it belonged to our grandmother, and she gave me my first lessons."

"We spent a lot of time around that piano when we were young," said Cousin William.

It was hard to imagine William ever being young. I figured he was one of those kids who always sat close to the teacher and wore a tie to school. He didn't look like he'd ever scuffed his shoes or gotten dirty on the playground.

"It needs tuning. All this humidity is the worst thing in the world for a piano. But one of these days Lucas will get it."

"I'd forgotten how hot it gets in South Georgia, Lettie." Cousin William waved a Duncan's Funeral Home fan in his face. "I don't think I could tolerate the heat down here now."

"When are we going to eat, Momma?" asked Robert, eyeing the candy box. "I'm hungry."

"Corinthia's gone to see her sister, but she made us some chicken salad and pimento cheese sandwiches. She didn't want to heat the kitchen up." She turned back to William and added, "We'll eat out on the back porch and you can see my flower garden."

"Do you still have the prettiest roses in Crisscross?" he asked.

"It's been awfully dry this spring—I only have six varieties this year. But the boys are good about keeping them watered."

Granny and Cousin William chatted about family news during lunch, and Robert and I listened in between helpings of chicken salad. Granny whispered to Robert to use his napkin and chew with his mouth closed. And I saw William frown when Robert picked a big chunk of white meat out of his back tooth and wiped his hands on his trousers.

I didn't say much until Cousin William asked me what I liked to study in school. After I told him history and English, he stroked his chin. "You seem like a smart boy. Have you ever thought about selling insurance?"

"I'm not sure what I'm going to do. I still have a couple more years of high school."

"Everyone needs insurance, Lucas. Believe it or not, some folks are worth more dead than alive." He laughed as if he'd just told us the funniest joke in the world. Adjusting his glasses, he added, "You can have a very successful career selling policies, and there's lots of benefits. In the past five years, Dorothy and I have traveled to meetings all over the country."

I liked the idea of traveling. But selling insurance and wearing a suit all day sounded pretty boring to me. "I'll remember that."

After lunch, Granny told Cousin William about all the folks who came to Paw Paw's funeral. Robert got fidgety and played with the string he always carried in his pocket, wrapping it around his head Indian style. He rocked back and forth in his chair, making silent war cries until Granny told him he could be excused. But I stayed on the porch while they talked.

"How are you going to get along without Harold?" Cousin William asked Granny as he helped himself to another piece of coconut cake.

"Little George is still here. He takes care of the fields and hires workers to help with the picking. He could run the place."

"And what about Alvin Earl?"

I stole a look at Granny, wondering if she'd mention Alvin Earl's drinking or poker games at Gordy's.

She brushed some crumbs from the table into a little pile and, without looking at William, said, "Alvin Earl is Alvin Earl. He still has a little house in Crisscross, but Harold left him the farm."

"I assumed he would. Have you met with his lawyer yet?

"We'll meet next week. I just couldn't bring myself to talk about the will right after the service."

"And the boys?" He gestured toward me.

"Oh, Lucas will be going to college in a couple of years. You know getting a good education is the best insurance you can have, and he's going to win a scholarship, aren't you, Lucas?"

"Yes, ma'am," I said, even though I wasn't sure my grades were good enough to get a scholarship.

"And what about Robert? Am I still his legal guardian?"

"Yes, you're the guardian for both boys. You're my closest relative."

I looked at Cousin William more closely. I knew he was Robert's guardian, but I didn't know he was also mine.

Cousin William stood up and cleared his throat like he was going to make a speech or something. Instead, he walked toward the porch steps. "I need to get back to Macon, but that was a real nice lunch, Lettie."

"It's been good to see you." Granny followed him to the steps.

Turning back to look at Granny, he abruptly stopped and lowered his voice. "What's going to happen to Robert as you get older?"

"I'm not going to get any older." Granny opened her eyes wide and shook her head back and forth. "He's going to stay right here on the farm with me."

"Have you considered putting him in some kind of home or the state hospital? He might be able to get some schooling and learn a simple skill."

"William, I've visited that hospital in Maysville and seen how they care for their patients. They either work them to death out in the fields or let them roam around the building all day in a stupor. They're dirty and the whole building smells like urine and feces."

Cousin William cleared his throat again. "I know a couple of men who serve on the board. It can't be that bad."

"It's worse. The staff is overworked and there's only a few doctors. And there's a security area with bars on all the windows and doors for convicted criminals."

"Criminals?"

"Yes—criminals of the worst kind—murderers and rapists and who knows what else? They've got a woman in there who poisoned two husbands and her mother-in-law with ant killer and arsenic. They arrested her when they caught her trying to poison her eleven-year-old daughter."

"Well, at least they're in a separate area," he said.

"That's what the admissions people say," said Granny, "but they sit in a nice, clean office all day. I don't think anyone really knows what goes on at that place."

I didn't say anything about what Cotton had told me about Maysville as Cousin William headed to his car. And I wondered if Granny knew about the suspicious deaths and bodies dumped out in a field.

## 21

A few days after Cousin William's visit, Robert and I were having a quiet breakfast in the kitchen. Corinthia had just put some hot eggs and grits on the table when the big black telephone in the hall rang. I heard Granny answer it and say, "Good morning, David."

Ten minutes later, she walked into the kitchen wearing her black funeral dress and patent leather shoes. "We're going into town this morning to see Mr. Barnett," she said, smoothing out her collar.

"Mr. Barnett, the lawyer?" I asked.

"Yes. He wants to discuss Paw Paw's will. Corinthia, will you ask Little George if he can drive us into Crisscross?"

"Are we going to see Daddy?" Robert asked in an excited voice.

Granny looked pained. "No, no. Your daddy's with the angels now, remember? Now go put on your Sunday shirts."

"We don't want y'all goin' into town all raggedy lookin'," said Corinthia. "Go on, now. I gonna go out to talk to Little George."

After Robert and I changed shirts, we went out to the back porch to wait for Granny. Little George stood by Paw Paw's old DeSoto, ready to go.

Granny took a quick sip of her coffee and hurried out to the porch. "Little George, come on up here for a minute. I want to tell you about a letter Mr. Harold wrote to you."

"A letter?" he asked, hobbling toward the porch.

"Yes—he wrote it right before he passed. I'll give it to you when you have more time to read it. Alvin Earl's going to meet us in Crisscross, and we're supposed to meet Mr. Barnett at 9:00."

"Yes, ma'am." Little George tipped his cap and stepped into the yard.

I remembered Paw Paw writing a letter to Little George right before he died, but I didn't think much about it. No one said much as we rode into town. And Granny didn't mention the letter again.

When we got closer to the square, she put on her white gloves and said, "I don't want y'all interrupting Mr. Barnett with lots of questions. Robert, don't play with that string in your pocket and don't touch anything in his office."

"Yes, ma'am," said Robert, and from the way he said it I could tell he didn't understand where we were going or remember who Mr. Barnett was.

Then Granny turned toward Little George and said, "Today you need to come in, too."

"You sure, Miz Lettie? I usually waits by the car."

"Mr. Harold's will mentions you," Granny said. "Robert, remember, I don't want you touching anything."

When we got to Mr. Barnett's office, Alvin Earl, looking like he'd slept in his clothes, was sitting in the waiting room. He hadn't shaved in a few days, and his shirt was stained with coffee.

The receptionist smiled and said, "Nice to see y'all. Mr. Barnett will be with you in a few minutes. Just have a seat."

The waiting room was cool and quiet. It was lined with books and file cabinets and smelled like tobacco. There were a couple of worn leather couches and end tables loaded with copies of *National Geographic* and *Time* magazines. I grabbed an old magazine with a picture of Roosevelt on the cover and sank onto the couch. The leather made a long, fart-like sound and Robert started giggling.

Putting his hand over his mouth, he whispered in a loud voice, "Lucas, that's not nice. You're supposed to say 'Excuse me.'"

I scowled at Robert. "That wasn't me—it was the couch."

"That was you," he insisted. "Say 'excuse me.'"

"Y'all quit being silly," said Granny, standing up. "Here comes Mr. Barnett."

"Morning, everyone. Morning, Alvin Earl." Mr. Barnett greeted us with a slight smile. "I'm sorry y'all are here under these circumstances. I thought a lot of Harold. He was one of my first clients and a good friend."

"Thank you, David," Granny said. "He thought a lot of you, too. He always said you were the best lawyer in South Georgia."

"Now, can we get started?" asked Alvin Earl. "I've got an appointment later today."

While Little George stood by the door like a guard on duty, we all took seats around Mr. Barnett's big glossy desk. Robert immediately reached for the old-fashioned inkwell with the shiny silver cap on the desk blotter. But after Granny shook her head at him, he pulled out his lucky penny and rolled it between his fingers. I stared at the collection of framed diplomas hanging on the wall and wondered how long it took Mr. Barnett to get all those degrees.

"I think y'all know," began Mr. Barnett as he cleaned his glasses with the tip of his tie, "that Harold left most of his property, including his dog Sam, and his assets to Alvin Earl. However, he did have a special provision for some of the acreage, and he also left a fund for Lucas's education."

"What are you talking about?" demanded Alvin Earl. "Daddy never said anything to me about a special provision or money for Lucas's education."

"Let him finish, Alvin Earl," said Granny.

"I never got any kind of money for an education." Alvin Earl glared at me. "And Lucas is no kin to Daddy or me. He's Miss Lettie's grandson—he doesn't even carry the family name."

"He may not be a blood relative, but at this time, he *is* the only grandchild." Mr. Barnett stressed the "is." "And Harold wanted him to have ample funds for his college tuition and books."

I didn't understand all the legal talk, but I wished Paw Paw had left me his old truck instead of an education fund. I needed some kind of transportation to school a lot more than I needed a college diploma.

Checking his watch, Mr. Barnett continued, "Alvin Earl, your father left two hundred and ten acres of the farm, which must remain intact, to you."

Alvin Earl shifted in his seat. "What do you mean intact?"

"Intact means that the land cannot be broken up. You can't sell ten or twenty acres off every few months without a special arrangement. May I continue?"

Alvin Earl buckled his arms across his chest like a big pretzel. "Yeah, but first tell me what happened to the other forty acres."

"Your father left forty acres in the backwoods to Little George."

"What?" He jumped up and slammed his fist on the desk. "Daddy had no business giving land to Little George. That land belongs to me."

"I never 'spected that," said Little George softly. "I been workin' for other folks mosta my life. Now I gots a chance to put in a crop on my own land."

"You ain't going to touch that land," Alvin Earl shouted.

"I believe Harold wanted to reward Little George for all of his years of service," Mr. Barnett said, pulling out a piece of paper from his stack of folders. "Here's the deed."

"Daddy must have been out of his mind. That's my land—I'm entitled to that land by birth." Alvin Earl snatched the deed from Mr. Barnett's hand.

"I don't determine how people divide up their property or assets. I merely make sure everything is done according to the laws of Georgia," Mr. Barnett said in a matter-of-fact voice. "Now, if you'll sit down, we can continue."

Alvin Earl lowered himself into his chair. Then he slowly tore the deed up, letting the pieces fall on Mr. Barnett's desk like confetti. "That paper ain't worth a bucket of you know what! I ain't giving up one inch of my land up to some gimpy nigger. I'm getting my own lawyer."

No one said a word or moved a muscle while Mr. Barnett brushed the scraps of paper off his desk with his sleeve and said, "That's your option and right. But you should be aware that I have another copy of the deed. Now let's continue."

Grumbling under his breath, Alvin Earl drummed his fingers on his armrests and shot Mr. Barnett a look of pure hate.

"As specified in the will, most of the income from the farm will go to you. However, you are expected to allow Miss Lettie, Robert, and Lucas to live on the property as long as they desire. Miss Lettie will receive funds for the salaries for Little George and Corinthia, and the purchase of seed, fertilizer, etc. She'll also have a fund for household expenses and repairs. I'll take the papers to the courthouse tomorrow. Does anyone have any more questions?"

"Yes," I said, raising my hand. "What happens to the special fund if I don't go to college? I might decide to go to a trade school or something."

"Oh, no. There's no question about your going to college," said Granny quickly. "We've planned on your going to college ever since you were a baby. Let's not take up any more of Mr. Barnett's time."

"Wait a minute!" broke in Alvin Earl. "I got a couple of questions. Who gets the farm if something happens to me?"

"If there are no heirs, Lucas will inherit all of the acreage and assets when he's of legal age," said Mr. Barnett, folding his hands on his desk.

"Lucas," snorted Alvin Earl. "What would he do with a farm?"

"That will be his decision. According to my notes, he's has been working on the farm since he was a small boy. Is that correct, Lucas?"

"Yes sir."

"And who gets the farm if something happens to Lucas?"

"The farm would go to Little George."

"Little George?" Alvin Earl jumped out of his chair again, his hands curling into fists. "Daddy don't owe that nigger a damn thing."

"As I said before, the will reflects your father's wishes."

Storming out the door, Alvin Earl shouted, "I'll see you in court."

## 22

As soon as we met with Mr. Barnett, everything changed. Alvin Earl moved back into his old room at Granny's with his guns and his stash of liquor. He swaggered around the farm like he was the richest man in South Georgia. Even before he was unpacked, he plastered a "No Trespassing" poster across the rusty Piano Lessons sign that had hung on a pole next to the mailbox since my mother was a girl.

"What are you doing?" asked Granny when she saw him covering her sign. "Folks still stop by to ask about lessons."

"I don't want to listen to some kid pounding on the piano, and I don't want anyone snooping around the place," he said.

"We've never had a problem with people snooping around," she said. "We don't even lock our doors."

"Well, y'all better start locking them now. There's a lot of crazy people running around the county."

Granny didn't argue with Alvin Earl about the No Trespassing sign, but she spent more time in her room whenever he was around. Robert and I spent more time in the fields and out in the shed. No one liked having Alvin Earl in the house.

He never seemed to do much on the farm except shout out orders day and night. He expected Corinthia to iron his shirts and his underwear a certain way and bring him food whenever he got hungry. When he was taking his afternoon nap, he insisted we all tiptoe around the house. And sometimes when I was out in the yard and heard him snoring, I'd sneak into his room and take a cigarette or two out of the pack he kept on his dresser just to spite him.

He got strange telephone calls late at night, and Corinthia said he was carrying on with women from all over the county. He hid bottles in his truck, and he'd come stumbling in late at night bumping into furniture and cussing. When I got up in the morning, I'd see cigarette butts on the porch and stuck in Granny's plants. He'd be passed out on his bed with a bottle of whiskey under his arm.

One Saturday afternoon after Robert and I had been out in the fields and just finished our lunch, I heard Alvin Earl stirring in his bedroom. He'd been out late the night before and yelled out, "Corinthia, quit banging all those pots and pans and bring me some coffee. I need coffee."

"Mr. Alvin Earl," called back Corinthia. "I gots all the breakfast stuff washed and put up and I doin' up the lunch dishes. It almost one o'clock."

"I got to have some coffee and biscuits. And I got to have it now," he said. "My head's pounding."

"I see what I can find," said Corinthia with a long sigh. Turning toward me, she grumbled, "That man think I runnin' some kinda restaurant."

"Hurry up, Corinthia," shouted Alvin Earl. "Your biscuits are going to be heavy enough to use as hubcaps on the old truck."

"Don't that man know I gots other things to do besides take his telephone messages and wait on him?" she asked. "He actin' like he king of the castle, but even a king can gets rat poison in their biscuits."

If Alvin Earl wasn't hounding Corinthia, he was finding fault with the way Little George handled Sam, cared for the mules, or managed the fields. His list went on and on. He tried to pick arguments over the slightest thing. If Little George said it was likely to rain, Alvin Earl would stare up at the sky like some kind of scientist and say, "Any fool can tell those ain't storm clouds." Little George never contradicted him, but he started coming to the farm earlier each morning and spent more time in the fields. He asked me to give Sam fresh water and food before I went to school.

Even though I tried to stay out of his way, Alvin Earl figured out a way to harass me, too. He'd barely finished high school and called me the Egg Head, telling me again and again that only the men who couldn't make it in the real world went to college. When I studied at the kitchen tables in the evenings, he'd turn the radio on full blast. Then he'd twist the knobs until the house was flooded with static, and he'd go out in the yard. When I turned the volume down, he'd come back in the house and say, "Oh, I didn't know you were doing your homework."

One night when I was finishing a final project that was forty percent of my English grade, he walked into the kitchen and deliberately spilled coffee on my paper. "Oh, golly darn, Lucas. Look what happened." He made a big show of blotting up the brown stain with his dirty handkerchief.

"Don't touch my paper," I said, pushing his hand away with my pencil.

"I'm so sorry," he said sarcastically. "You must have been working on something real important—we all know how smart you are."

"I'm smart enough to know when someone tries to ruin my project on purpose."

"What are you saying?" he asked in an innocent voice.

"You figure it out." I gathered up my papers and switched off the lights, leaving him alone in the dark.

But he treated Robert worse than anyone and loved to torment him about killing off his chickens. If no one was around, he'd tell Robert he was going to have Corinthia cut off Flossie's head. While Robert watched, she'd bleed her out in the backyard and fry her up for Sunday supper. Then Alvin Earl would tell him Corinthia was going to do the same thing with Sugar Pie and the rest of his hens. As Robert started to cry and scream in protest, a cruel grin would cross Alvin Earl's face and he'd say, "We'll eat up all your pets by the end of the summer."

If I asked why he was being so mean to Robert, he'd call me a smartass and deny everything he said about killing off the hens. He'd tell me I was just making things up.

When Alvin Earl wasn't tormenting Robert, he tried to work him to death. Robert had always collected the eggs and helped in Granny's garden. But now, despite Granny's objections, Alvin Earl made him work in the fields and take care of the mules. After he gave Jewel and Molly fresh hay every day, he had to bring them six or seven buckets of water. Then he had to shovel out their stalls. When Little George and Cotton tried to help him, Alvin Earl would say, "That boy's got to make himself useful around here. If he doesn't want to work like everybody else, I'll send him to the state hospital."

He called Robert a moron when Granny wasn't around. To his face, he called him dimwit or four-eyes. He didn't have any table manners, but he got furious when Robert slurped his food and smacked his lips while we were eating. He made fun of his stubby fingers and the way he held his silverware and struggled with his buttons and zippers.

One Friday when Robert and I were eating a sandwich with Granny and Corinthia was ironing, Alvin Earl came into the kitchen. Pointing to Robert's crotch, he said, "Zip up your pants, boy! No one wants to see your puny little pecker hanging out." Slapping me on the back, he looked at me as if we were best buddies. "It would be different if you had a nice big pecker like mine or Lucas's—right, Lucas? Women would pay to see that."

Even though Alvin Earl's voice sounded friendly, I knew he was mocking me. I blushed and prayed Robert wouldn't say anything about Amelia. But Robert clutched his crotch and giggled. Dropping his eyes, he fumbled with his zipper, trying to close his fly.

Granny's face turned whiter than Corinthia's apron. She stepped in front of Robert as if she were trying to protect him and said, "Alvin Earl, we don't use that kind of language in this house."

"You better remember whose house this is before you get so high and mighty." He deliberately struck a match on the kitchen table and lit a cigarette. Leaning toward Granny, he exhaled in her face.

"Owning property doesn't give you or anyone else the right to use bad language and bully people." Granny grabbed Robert's hand. "Let's go sit on the back porch where we can get some fresh air and a breeze."

"Ohhh," whispered Corinthia to me. "Miz Lettie givin' it back to Alvin Earl now. She ain't gonna listen to that trash mouth."

"No one wants to listen to Alvin Earl," I said.

I tried to ignore him the same way I ignored the Overtons when they taunted me on the bus. And I told Robert to ignore him. But the longer Alvin Earl was around the farm, the harder it was to ignore him.

## 23

Alvin Earl was gone when I got up early the next morning, and Little George and Corinthia had gone into town. I grabbed a biscuit off the table and hurried out to the kennel to feed Sam. I knew Sam missed seeing Little George, but he was glad to get his breakfast.

Robert stood on the porch steps watching me and called, "I'm going to hide. Come find me, Lucas."

"I'm taking care of Sam."

"Come find me!" he called again.

"Sam needs more water." I stalled, grabbing the bucket and then putting the bag of food back in the shed. I wandered toward the pump house, expecting Robert to be in his usual hiding place. But there was no sign of him.

Surprised, I looked all over the backyard and walked back toward the shed. "Where are you?" I called. "Come on now. We've got lots of chores this morning. I haven't got all day to look for you."

Robert can't do anything right, I thought. He can't even play a simple game of hide-and-seek. I figured he was probably out in the woods behind the barn where J.T. and I found an arrowhead. Following an overgrown path, I spotted a hawk circling overhead and moved deeper into the woods.

Little George had taught me the names of lots of trees and plants and their uses. But I wasn't interested in the wild azaleas and flowering dogwoods this morning. It was already hot, and the mosquitoes were as thick as Air Force bombers. Sweat rolled down my back, sticking to my shirt. I wanted to find Robert and get back home before Granny noticed we were gone.

I trudged through the brambles and prickly weeds, calling his name. I saw a jagged wire fence that had once marked a cotton field and passed a rusty No Hunting sign nailed to a dying tree. Ducking low-hanging limbs, I tripped on some tangled roots and hoped I wouldn't see or hear any snakes. Last year, Little George used a shovel to kill a rattlesnake with fourteen rattles in the backwoods. But everything was quiet except for the caws from a couple of crows and the rustle of a squirrel scampering through the leaves.

The air felt heavy. I caught the odor of leaf mold and rot. Briars tore at my pant legs, and small patches of sunlight flickered on the ground. I kept shouting, "Robert, Roberrrt," and then I suddenly realized that something could have happened to him. He didn't have his glasses, and he couldn't see much far away.

I started getting panicky. I thought of all the times I'd been impatient and short-tempered with him when he tagged along with me. Robert never went anywhere alone. After the fire in the bedroom, Granny was scared to let him out of her sight. Most people couldn't understand him, and even if they did, he couldn't remember our phone number or where we lived.

A couple of years ago, he'd gotten lost when Paw Paw and Granny took us to the Southeastern Farm Show in Macon. After the cattle auction, we went to the fishing pond booth so Robert could try to win a Kewpie doll with a red cap and rifle. Granny paid a dime for each try, but the only thing he won was a game of Jacks.

When we headed back to the big tent to watch the next auction, the midway was packed with people. Somehow Robert got separated from us. Granny got hysterical. A deputy helped us look for him. We finally found him standing by the cotton candy machine, crying so hard he couldn't even say his name.

If I couldn't find Robert, Granny would call Sheriff Norton, and he'd call for local volunteers. The sheriff would organize a search party because Robert had disappeared when I was supposed to be watching him. And if anything happened to him, Granny would never forgive me.

"Robert, Roberrrt!" My voice was getting hoarse from shouting his name. I picked up a rock and threw it at a tree. "Quit playing around. Answer me!"

Swatting away the mosquitoes, I kept walking and noticed fresh deer tracks leading to a clearing. I heard a turkey call and saw the pond where we fished. As I got closer, Jesus bugs skimmed across the water and I could make out ripples of circles from a fish breaking the surface. Then I heard someone calling my name.

"Lucas, Lucas!"

"Robert, is that you?" I spotted a stocky figure waving his arms on the far side of the pond. I shook my head in disbelief.

"Lucas, I'm here!" He ran around the edge of the water and rushed toward me. Crying, he hugged me so hard I almost lost my balance. His face was dirty and his hair was stuck to his head with sweat. His shoes were caked with mud and his shirt was torn. And he had long red scratch marks on his arm from picking at his mole.

"What are you doing out here? You know you're not supposed to leave the yard."

"You told me to hide someplace different." His lower lip trembled and he fingered the hole in his shirt.

"I told you that months ago." My voice was low and angry. I couldn't believe he could remember what I'd said about getting a new hiding place back in the spring—but couldn't remember his address or how much two plus three was.

He nodded. "I did what you said."

"Did you get lost?"

"I waited, but you didn't come. And I was all by myself." Starting to cry again, he blew his nose in the palm of his hand. Then he wiped his hand on his overalls and pulled at the tear in his shirt, making it worse.

"Don't pull on your shirt! You're okay now. But you can't just run off by yourself."

"I know." Robert buried his face in my shoulder and clung to my arm, digging his fingers into my flesh.

"Quit! You're getting snot all over me." I shook him off my shoulder. "Let's go back to the house. Don't say anything to Granny or anyone else about getting lost this morning. Do you understand?"

"Okay, Lucas," Robert sniffled, dragging his arm across his nose. "I won't say anything."

"It'll be our secret. You remember what a secret is?"

Robert put his finger to his lips and smiled, acting like we had a new game.

"Right, now get your face wiped off."

## 24

Early the next Sunday morning while I was lying in bed listening to the train whistle in the distance and Robert's puffy snore, I heard Alvin Earl's truck tearing up the driveway. But instead of parking in the gravel area next to the house, he pulled into the front yard and braked by the porch. I waited to hear the door slam and his heavy footsteps in the parlor, but the house was quiet.

A few minutes later, our bedroom door opened and Granny, wearing her nightgown and robe, slipped into the room. Standing by my bed, she whispered, "Lucas, wake up, wake up. Alvin Earl just came home and he's out in the yard."

"What? What time is it?" I asked, trying to figure out what was going on.

"It's around 4:00. And Alvin Earl's truck's out front—he's lying in the grass. I need you to help me get him into the house."

"Just let him stay there," I mumbled, putting my pillow over my head. "I'm sleeping."

"No, no, get up!" She leaned toward me, tugging at the pillow. "I don't want any of the neighbors to see him on their way to church. You know the Jenkins always go to the 8:30 service."

"What difference does it make? Everyone in Crisscross knows he's a drunk."

"Shhh. Don't wake up Robert." She grabbed my pillow. "It makes a difference to me, and someday it could make a difference to you."

Pulling on my sheet, I snatched my pillow back and heard Robert stir. "Why? Alvin Earl's no kin to me. I'm going back to sleep."

"I need your help, but I'm not going to argue with you, Lucas."

"I'm awake, Momma. I'll help you." Robert sat up in his bed. "I'm strong."

"You're my good boy." Granny turned on my desk lamp. "Put your pants and slippers on and we'll get him in the house. Don't worry about your zipper."

Robert pulled on his pants and hurried out the door behind Granny. I was wide awake by now and slid out of bed to peek through the open window. There wasn't much of a moon, so Granny flipped on the porch light. I could see Alvin Earl stretched out on his back with his head and shoulders slumped against one of Granny's big half-barrel planters of roses. His eyes were closed, and his shirt was torn and bloody. It looked like he had a package of Camels clutched in his hand.

"I'll hold the door, Robert. You get him up out of the yard and up the stairs," Granny said.

"Alvin Earl, Alvin Earl," said Robert, stooping down next to him.

Alvin Earl grunted.

"Get up, come on, get up." Robert grabbed his arm and struggled to pull him to his feet. "Momma wants you to come in the house."

"Keep away from me, you moron! I don't need your help. I don't need anybody's help." He reached out to hit Robert, but his arm flopped to his side like a dead fish.

He rolled onto his hip and got to his knees. Bracing himself against the planter, he got himself up and stumbled toward the house. When he got to the front steps, I saw a nasty gash on his cheek and a bruise running across his forehead. He staggered and reached for the railing, pulling himself up the stairs one foot at a time like a cripple. But when he got to the top of the stairs, he lost his grip on the metal bar. "I'm sick, real sick." Then he collapsed on his stomach on the steps.

"I think he's passed out." Granny moved toward the steps. "Maybe we can roll him over."

"He stinks," said Robert, holding his nose.

"Just cover him with a blanket," I called through the window. "And stick a few of your roses on it so he doesn't smell."

"I don't have time to listen to your foolishness," called back Granny, pushing on Alvin Earl's arm. "Just go back to bed if you're not going to help."

Ashamed of myself, I threw on my pants and shoes. I hurried out to the porch. "All right, Granny. We'll get him in the house. You hold the door."

Standing on the top step, I stuck my foot under Alvin Earl's shoulder and tried to roll him over on his back. But trying to move him was like trying to move the old anvil out in the barn.

"Get up, Alvin Earl. Come on, get up." I kicked his butt a couple of times. "I want to get back to bed."

"Leave me alone," he moaned. "Where's Betty Jean?" Moaning again, he managed to get to his hands and knees and crawl the rest of the way up the steps.

"Betty Jean left a couple of years ago. Now stand up!"

"I never should have let her go."

"That's right. Not many people would want to live with you."

"What are you talking about?" He lurched forward and gasped, "I'm sick—I'm going to puke."

He wretched, heaving up something that looked like a brown river with big chunks of pretzels and hot dogs floating on top of it. When he finished, he wiped his mouth with his sleeve. "I need some water." He fell back on his butt, his legs stuck out in front of him and his eyes locked shut. And the vomit pooled up under Granny's favorite rocking chair.

"This smells real bad. Don't step in it, Robert." My stomach turned inside out and I tried not to gag.

Granny stood by the screen door, turning her head in disgust. "It's all over the porch. Just get him inside. I'll help you."

"Leave me alone," he whined. "I'm sick."

"Prop the door open, Granny. Robert, grab one of his boots," I said, barely able to speak. "I'll get the other one. Swing him around toward the door and we'll drag him in the house."

"Ohhhh." Robert jerked his hand back. "He's got throw up on his boots and his shirt."

Pulling and panting, we dragged him off the porch and got him through the front door into the old parlor.

"Let's get him into his bedroom," said Granny, wiping her hands on an old kitchen towel.

"I'm not touching him again, Granny. He can lie in the middle of the floor forever for all I care." I grabbed the towel and promised myself I'd never get drunk enough to get sick and vomit. All I wanted to do was wash myself off to get rid of that smell and go back to bed.

"I'm glad his daddy isn't around to see this. He's worse now than he ever was." Granny shook her head.

"So why don't you kick him out? Why are you putting up with him?"

"I can't kick him out, Lucas." Granny sighed and sank into a chair, rubbing her temples. "Remember, this is his house now."

"Let's move. We don't have to stay here, do we?"

"Where are we going to go? Do you want to move into town with Robert?"

"I don't care where we go—we just want to get away from Alvin Earl. Don't we, Robert?"

"Yeah, he smells bad and he's mean. He calls me MOR-ON," said Robert, wiping his hands on his pants.

A long minute passed before Granny sighed again. Looking at Robert and then me, she said, "I don't think there's much I can do, but I'll talk with Mr. Barnett."

"Mr. Barnett's not the only lawyer around. Somebody's got to be able to help us get Alvin Earl out of the house," I said.

"We'll start with Mr. Barnett. Now let's get a couple of buckets and wash down the porch."

"You get the buckets, Robert, and I'll move his truck and clean up the yard." Being careful not to touch Alvin Earl's shirt, I reached in his pants pocket and found his keys. "This is probably the only time I'll get to drive it."

I went out in the yard, thankful to breathe in the clean air. I picked up the cigarettes in the grass, hoping I'd find a couple to smoke. I heard the trill of a screech owl near the barn and headed toward his truck. It was caked with dust and grit, and the seat was littered with empty Camel packs and crumpled scraps of paper.

When I smoothed out the papers in the early light, I realized they were IOUs signed by Alvin Earl. The names and amounts were smudged, but I stuck them in my pocket, wondering how much money he owed. As I cranked up the engine, I recognized the sound of Cotton's muffler. When I parked, he coasted into the spot next to me and hopped out.

"Did Alvin Earl make it home?" he asked, leaning against his hood and lighting up a cigarette.

"Yeah, but he looked pretty bad." I cut off the engine and got out, slamming the door as hard as I could, knowing I'd have to wash and wax the truck tomorrow. "He puked all over the front porch and then he passed out. We had to pull him in the house."

"You and Robert?" Cotton chuckled and blew a smoke ring. "Wish I coulda seed that."

"It wasn't easy. Robert's strong, but Alvin Earl weighs over two hundred pounds."

"He had a lot to drink 'fore he started playin' and got in a fight at Gordy's."

"What happened?" I asked, bumming a drag from his cigarette.

"He lost a lota money and say the little guy at his table usin' a loaded deck. He jump up and start punchin' him in the face. It look like he broke his jaw. 'Fore you know it, everybody at his table throwin' punches. I just 'bout ready to pull out my ice pick."

"Did he knock the little guy out?"

"No, but his face all covered in blood. Things finally settles down and Gordy tell Alvin Earl to get out 'fore they calls the sheriff."

"Did everybody leave?" I asked.

"Just Alvin Earl—he took off like somebody just yell fire. He jump in his truck and almost back into a light pole. He real lucky the sheriff not 'round tonight."

I took another drag, holding the smoke deep in my lungs. "Were the men at Gordy's from somewhere around here? Did you know them?"

"No! They big-time gamblers from Atlanta and up north somewhere. They way outa his league."

"Well, he ain't got any cash—things are still tied up with the bank."

"Those mens ain't gonna take credit. And they ain't gonna wait 'round. They be gettin' morea their friends and huntin' him down like a wild boar." Cotton finished his cigarette and dropped his butt, grinding it into the gravel with the toe of his boot. "How long 'fore he get some cash?"

"I don't know. He might end up going to court."

"You think he look bad tonight? He gonna look real bad if those mens and their friends come 'round here and he don't pay up."

Patting the IOUs in my pocket, I said, "I guess he's going to have to sell that fancy truck or hide out somewhere."

## 25

Alvin Earl disappeared for more than a week after he tore up the front yard with his truck and passed out on the porch. Cotton said he was probably staying with his lady friend near Macon. I didn't care where he was as long as he was gone. Robert and I still did all our chores, but we could breathe a little easier while he was away. In the evenings, we relaxed on the back porch and watched the fireflies. I listened to the ball games or mystery theater on the old radio and hoped Alvin Earl would stay gone for good.

In the mornings, while Little George was feeding the mules, I took Sam for a run just to keep him from getting fat. But when the temperatures hit the nineties by eight, Sam didn't feel much like doing much running and neither did I.

"All Sam wants to do is lie around in his pen and sleep," I told Little George one day while he was cleaning out a stall.

"He just hot like the rest of us." Little George rested on his shovel and stretched his good leg. "He get more active like when it get close to huntin' season."

"Cotton says he's getting old." I wiped my forehead with my shirttail.

"He perk up when it start coolin' off. You wait and see. I gonna start workin' him in the next week or two just to make sure he sharp. Maybe you help me."

But before Little George and I could start working with him, Sam disappeared. When we were getting ready for church the next Sunday, I looked out the kitchen window and saw an empty kennel. The door was wide open and he was gone.

"Sam, Sam!" I called, racing out to the yard. Robert followed behind me. "Where are you?" I ran to the barn and shed, but didn't see any trace of Sam.

"Where is he?" asked Robert.

"I don't know," I said. "Look around the garden. I'm going to look along the road."

I ran along the road all the way to the state route junction, calling for Sam. But the only thing I saw was a flock of wild turkeys that scattered as soon as they spotted me. Turning around, I ran back to the house and told Granny that Sam was gone.

"Y'all looked out by the shed and the barn?" she asked.

"We even looked by the old privy, and I checked the road."

She grabbed her garden hat. "Well, let's look again. We've got to find him before Alvin Earl gets back." The three of us circled the yard and front field calling for Sam.

"He couldn't have gone too far," I said. "He hasn't been fed today and I know he'll be hungry. I'm going to look in the outer fields and backwoods. Robert, you stay here and help Granny."

I cut through the outer fields and pines to the fishing pond, calling Sam's name. The sun rose high and my shirt was plastered to my back. I tripped on a root and went sprawling head first into a bunch of briars, scratching my cheek. Cursing, I swung back toward the house and walked along the road for another couple of miles. But Sam was no-where to be seen.

"He's gone," I reported to Granny. "I didn't see any tire tracks in the yard, but someone must have picked him up. Alvin Earl's No Trespassing sign didn't do much good."

"Did you look along the road and see if someone hit him?"

I nodded, glad that I hadn't found bits and pieces of him smeared between the gravel.

"Rinse off that cut and get the truck. We'll go tell Little George. If anyone can find Sam, it'll be Little George."

We squeezed into the front seat of Paw Paw's old truck. Bouncing along the dirt road to the colored section of Criss-cross, I hoped the radiator wouldn't overheat. I drove quickly, and for once, Granny didn't watch the speedometer.

In all the years I'd lived with Granny and Paw Paw, I'd only been to Little George's house a few times. It was one of the few homes with a mowed yard and flower beds with roses and azaleas. When we pulled up, Corinthia and Little George were sitting in the rockers on their front porch.

"Mornin'," Little George called out. "What y'all doin' out so early on a Sunday?"

"Sam's gone—we've been out looking for him," I said.

"That how you cut yourself, Lucas?" asked Corinthia, studying my face as I got out of the truck.

"I got caught up in some briars and fell in the woods by the crossroads."

"How long he been gone?" Standing up, Little George jingled his keys.

"He was in his kennel when we went to bed. Someone must have taken him late last night," I said, rubbing my cheek.

"Let me get my truck and I follows you back to the farm," he said. "We fin' him."

"Y'all better fin' him. Alvin Earl skin those boys 'live if that dog disappear," said Corinthia.

"He better not touch me," I said.

"If Sam gone, y'all better stay outa his way cuz he gonna wanna go after somebody," said Little George, revving up the engine.

We searched the fields and backwoods again for a couple of hours. But Sam was nowhere to be found.

"That dog disappear like Houdini," said Little George. "Somebody done took him."

When Alvin Earl came home the next day and saw the empty kennel, his face turned purple and the veins in his neck bulged out. He kicked the pen with his heavy boots. "You went off and left that gate open, didn't you?" He grabbed my arm and spun me around toward him like a toy top. "You ain't got any more sense than that idiot Robert."

"I didn't leave the gate open," I snapped, jerking my arm away. "I know to close it up."

127

"Don't lie to me!" He lunged toward me, pushing his finger in my face. "I hate liars."

"I ain't a liar. I closed the gate."

"You didn't hear him barking or anyone coming into the yard?"

"I was sleeping. And I'm used to hearing him bark at night."

Turning toward Little George, Alvin Earl asked in a gruff voice, "So where is he?"

"No tellin', Mr. Alvin Earl," said Little George. "We've been lookin' for him almost two days—we even went out to the backwoods and up and down the county road. But he gone."

"Gone? Where'd he go?"

"I think somebody musta took him real early Sunday mornin'. The house real quiet and they figure everybody sleepin'."

"Took him? How could somebody take a dog like Sam?"

"They comes 'round and toss him big chunks of meat real friendly like."

Alvin Earl glared at Little George. "How do I know you didn't take that dog to try and sell? He'd follow you anywhere."

Little George's eyes flashed and he sucked his breath in through his teeth. "I be workin' on this farm for over twenty-five years. Why would I take Sam? I helped raise him up from a pup."

"Men steal dogs and then collect the reward from the owner. It's easy money."

"Dogs always disappear before hunting season starts," I said. "Everyone knows that."

"Yeah, and it's usually some niggers that finds 'em," said Alvin Earl, stressing *finds*. "I heard Cotton found a dog a while back and got a lot of money. He probably—"

"You heard wrong. Cotton wouldn't take Sam," I interrupted.

Little George took a deep breath and stared straight ahead. "My momma and daddy didn't raise us up to steal. Nobody in my family ever took a huntin' dog to get the reward. There likely somebody else 'round here pickin' up dogs to collect the money."

I didn't say anything, but I knew Little George was thinking about that sorry Horace Overton, the twins' father. He spent most of his time at Gordy's and collected a relief check every week. Everyone in Crisscross knew Horace and the twins hunted out of season. But no one ever reported them to the game warden since they knew the kids ate whatever they shot.

"I'm going to keep my eyes open and offer a reward," said Alvin Earl, puffing out his chest and hooking his thumbs on his belt like a cowboy from a Western. "I'll tell you one thing, whoever took Sam will be sorry. He'll wish he never set foot on my property."

## 26

Cotton and I posted reward signs in town, and for the next couple of weeks we drove around the county asking about Sam. A lot of folks had heard about Paw Paw's champion pointer, but no one had seen him. And I figured he was long gone.

The days grew longer and it was hot enough to melt your britches. We settled into our summer routine while Alvin Earl was in and out. Robert and I worked in the fields with Little

George and Cotton, waiting for the first blooms on the cotton.

One day when Little George and Corinthia took Granny and Robert into town for a doctor's appointment, I was supposed to rake out Granny's azalea beds and cut the front yard. I worked for about an hour in the glaring sun and decided to take a break on the porch. While I was sitting on the swing watching a dirt dauber build its tunnel in the eaves, a brand new blue Buick with whitewalls cruised by the house. Even with the dust on the tires, the car looked like it had just rolled out of the factory. The front grill gleamed like a row of new quarters.

It had Georgia plates, and the driver wore a black cowboy hat about the size of Hopalong Cassidy's. He went on down the county road, looping around so he could drive by the house again. When he got closer to our mailbox, he slowed down and parked the car across the road as if that grassy strip was his special spot. He got out and glanced up and down the road. Then, with his back to the house, he took a long piss next to a rusty fence post.

Turning around, he zipped up his blue jeans and leaned against his front fender as he stared at our front porch. He was a short, stocky man with powerful shoulders, and he wore boots with stacked heels and pointed toes. I wondered if he had a six-shooter tucked under the seat of the Buick.

Grabbing my rake, I ran into the front yard and called, "Hey, mister, this ain't a public bathroom. You're on private property. Don't you see the No Trespassing sign?"

He took a couple of steps toward the house and said, "What did you say, Sonny?" After a few seconds, he crossed the road and stood on the gravel walk leading to the front steps. Flicking his eyes toward me, he pulled a bottle out of his hip pocket. He unscrewed the lid and took a couple of swallows. And I realized he was one of the men who was in the yard with Alvin Earl at Paw Paw's funeral.

"My name's not Sonny. And I said you're on private property. Go somewhere else to do your business."

"You own this road?" he snarled.

"We own that fence and over two hundred acres on both sides of the road. Do you want to see the deed?"

He took another step forward and stuck the bottle back in his pocket. For a moment I was afraid he'd come after me. But instead he stopped and surveyed the yard as if he were trying to memorize every tree and shrub.

"Alvin Earl told me he owned this farm now. Who are you?" he demanded, pushing back the rim of his hat and squinting at me.

"I'm kind of like his nephew."

"Nephew?" He snorted again and scratched the hairs sticking out around his collar. "The only family I knew about was some half-wit brother. Where's your uncle?"

"He's my step-uncle—I don't know where he is." Gripping my rake, I wondered when Little George would be back.

"He's probably over in Macon," the man said, rocking back in his boots. "You know he's staying with some whore over there?"

"That's his business. I don't keep up with him and he don't keep up with me."

"If he ain't got any money, she'll get tired of him hanging around real quick." He craned his neck to look toward the backyard. "You here by yourself?"

"No, our hired man is out in the barn," I lied. "And the postman's on his way." I twisted my head around, straining to see the mail truck. I was relieved to see the red flag up on the metal box.

He stared down the road and placed his beefy hand on the box. Shifting his eyes toward me, he put the flag down. "Oh, yeah? Well, I need to talk with Alvin Earl."

"I told you he's not here. I don't know when he'll be back." My voice came out like a raspy whisper.

"When he does get back, you tell him Gus was here."

"Gus?" I repeated stupidly, staring at his pointy-toed boots.

"Yeah, Gus." He reached in his pocket and pulled out a pair of brass knuckles. Smiling, he slipped them on his hand, the metal glittering in the sunlight. "Does that name mean anything to you?"

I shook my head, but I knew he was one of the men from Gordy's that Cotton had told me about. And I wondered how much money Alvin Earl owed him.

"Your step-uncle knows who I am and what I want. And he knows I'll be back if I don't get it."

Without saying another word, he slowly headed toward his car and got in. He cranked his engine and took off toward Crisscross, leaving me standing alone by the house.

Later that day, I checked the spot where he'd pissed to see if the grass had turned brown. It hadn't, and Alvin Earl didn't come home for supper. I didn't say anything to anyone about Gus's visit. But I kept my eye out for the blue Buick with white sidewalls.

It must have been over one hundred degrees in our room that night, even with the windows open. I tossed and turned, dozing on and off. When I finally fell asleep, I dreamed I heard a man following me in the woods. I couldn't see his face, but I started to run, searching for a cave or someplace to hide. I ran and ran, long limbs and briars tearing at my arms and clothes. The man was getting closer and I could hear his heavy breathing. I came to a cliff as it was getting dark. Turning around, I picked up a big rock to throw it in his face. But before I could throw it, I stumbled and fell off the edge of the cliff. As I hurled toward the bottom of the ravine, I woke myself up, sweating and panting.

## 27

The sun was low in the sky when Alvin Earl came home a few days later. We were all sitting on the back porch listening to the ball game, and Little George was out in the shed stacking wood. I could still see the purple bruise on Alvin Earl's forehead and the long scab on his cheek from the fight at Gordy's.

But I could tell he was in a good mood when he called out, "Y'all come and see my new setter. She's gonna make me a rich man."

Little George limped over to the gravel lot and helped Alvin Earl unload a rusty crate. Alvin Earl opened the door, and we moved closer to get a good look at his new dog.

"Her name is Lady Luck—I won her in a card game and she has a stack of papers as long as my arm," he said proudly. "Her line goes all the way back to some breeder in England."

She was a lot smaller than Sam and had a white wavy coat with tan markings. But she huddled in the back of the crate like she was afraid someone was going to beat her.

"It's okay, girl," I said softly, stooping down to get a better look at the trembling dog. "No one's going to hurt you."

"Get out of there, Lady," Alvin Earl said, grabbing her collar. As he pulled her out, she stiffened her legs, her nails scraping against the metal. "Come on now, get out."

"She just a pup," Little George said. "She gots a real pretty head, but she sure need a good brush."

"She looks nice," Robert said, reaching out to touch her. "Just like Lassie."

Lady shied away from Robert and moved back toward the crate.

Without taking his eyes off the dog, Little George said, "Let her be, now. She kinda skittish cuz she in a new place. She gotta get use' to us."

"When she comes in season, I'm gonna breed her and sell each of her pups for $75," Alvin Earl said.

"That's a lot of money." I knelt next to the dog and held out my hand for her to sniff. I could buy two scooters and some new tires with $75.

"She is pretty, but who can pay $75 for a puppy? No one has that kind of money nowadays," Granny said.

"People come from all over the state to hunt in Treble County," Alvin Earl said. "Some of those big company men from Albany and Atlanta can pay $75 and more."

"There's still lots of men looking for jobs," Granny said.

"How do you know?" he demanded, his mood darkening. "How many times have you been to the big city?" Granny squeezed her eyes tight, but she didn't say a word to Alvin Earl.

"She goes to Columbia every year to visit her cousin William," I blurted out.

"I know all about William and his big insurance company," Alvin Earl said with a sneer. "And I've heard all about his fancy house in Columbia."

Granny frowned and silently shushed me. Alvin Earl turned to Robert. "Get all that crap out of Sam's old kennel, boy, and put in some fresh straw." Then he pulled out some new brushes from the truck bed and tossed them at me. "Lucas, I want you to groom Lady every day and keep all the burrs out. Little George will show you how. Don't let that boy touch her."

"Come on, girl." I reached for Lady's leash. "We'll get you all fixed up in your new pen. I'll put a bell on your gate so we know if anyone comes around at night."

"I'm going to take her out hunting tomorrow."

"I don't believe the season open yet," Little George said. "And we gots a new game warden."

"Folks say he's pretty strict about regulations and checks for licenses," I added, letting Lady sniff my hand. "He'll fine you even if you're on your own property."

"Nobody's been around here for a couple of months," Alvin Earl said. "The warden'll never know."

Alvin Earl was fined for hunting out of season two years ago, and last year he shot more birds than the legal bag limit. He told his daddy he'd gotten some extra birds from his friends. Paw Paw didn't say anything, but I knew he'd been hunting by himself and Paw Paw did, too.

The next day, Alvin Earl headed out with Lady in the back of his truck. They weren't gone very long before I heard his truck roaring up the drive and Lady howling. When he came stomping back toward the kennel, he was dragging her on a tight leash. And he had a handkerchief spotted with blood wrapped around his knuckles.

"Don't you pull away from me," he snarled, kicking her with his heavy boot.

Lady yelped, her tail tucked between her legs. I winced. "Don't kick her. She's still a pup."

Glaring at me, he tossed her leash at Little George as if it were a hot wire. "Take her. She roots around in the field and runs up the birds. She's no good with commands. When I tried to bring her in, she nipped at me." He held out his hand for us to look at in case we didn't believe him.

"I sees that." Little George picked up Lady's leash.

"Work her and get her ready for the first of the season," Alvin Earl instructed, massaging his bandaged hand. "If she don't listen, pull her ears and twist them or beat her. I don't care what you do. I can't make any money breeding a stubborn setter."

"I trained all kinda dogs, Mr. Alvin Earl. She gonna be fine."

"Don't feed her much. Hunting dogs work better when they're hungry."

"I don't know 'bout that," said Little George, patting Lady's head. "She just need a little practice and—"

"You can give her water," interrupted Alvin Earl, "but keep her lean."

"You want him to beat her and starve her?" I demanded. Little George caught my eye and shook his head, sending me a silent warning.

"This is none of your business," growled Alvin Earl. "She's my dog."

"Dogs are just like people. Beating a dog and starving it just makes it mean." The words came out in a rush and I avoided looking at Little George.

"You don't even like to hunt, smartass. What do you know?" Alvin Earl's eyes narrowed to slits, and he looked like he wanted to punch me in the mouth.

"I know a lot more than you think," I said.

"We'll see about that," said Alvin Earl, heading toward his truck.

As soon as Alvin Earl drove off, Little George gave Lady a quick pat. He let her off the leash and she wandered around the yard.

"Look, she tryin' to pick up a scent. Mr. Alvin Earl in too much of a hurry. He don't need to be starvin' her."

"And he doesn't need to twist her ears or beat her," I added, watching her sniffing Granny's azaleas.

## 28

Little George didn't do much with Lady for the next couple of days. But he spent a lot of time watching her trying to pick up a scent in the yard and rubbing her head with his large hands. He wanted her to get used to him so she would listen for his voice.

I brushed her every day, making sure her coat was smooth and silky. If Alvin Earl was gone, Robert would help me. She was a sweet dog, and I called her Lady Love. As soon as I walked across the yard, her feathery tail started going like Granny's metronome on high speed. When I whistled, she raced to me, ready to go. And I thought she was a lot easier to get along with than most folks I knew.

I made her a special collar out of an old leather strip and carved her name on it with my pocketknife. Even though she wasn't supposed to eat table scraps, I smuggled bits of sausage and biscuit out of the kitchen for her. She'd gently lick my fingers when she finished as if she were telling me thank you.

Little George knew I was feeding her biscuits and one day asked, "Who trainin' who, Lucas? Now she 'spectin' somethin' special to eat every time she see you." Chuckling, he reminded me every day that she wasn't a pet, but he never said I couldn't give her treats.

After a few days, Little George slipped a long check cord made out of a bale string around Lady's neck and gave her some basic commands. Over the next ten days, they practiced heel, hunt birds, and whoa. If she didn't obey, he'd pull up on the cord or step on it. When she obeyed his command, he praised her and rubbed her head. Sometimes he'd give her a little piece of sausage.

Cotton and I watched him work her one morning while Cotton was checking the spark plugs on the tractor. "She comin' 'long real good," Cotton said, looking for a wrench. "Little George can train just 'bout anything with four legs and half a brain."

"Maybe he needs to train Alvin Earl," I said, handing Cotton a wrench.

"That man don't need trainin'. He need to be on a leash and tied to a tree."

"Yeah. Lady never tried to bite Little George or me," I agreed.

"This dog wouldn't take a bite out of a biscuit if you didn't feed it to her," said Cotton. "But she do like to play."

"Yep, she'd go after a couple of rolled-up socks or a ball all day," I said. "She even went after one of your old base-balls."

Just then, Alvin Earl walked out in the yard with a ciga-rette in his hand and called out, "That dog better be going after birds—not balls. Is she ready for the first of the season?"

"She still need some practice, but she gonna be a fine huntin' dog," Little George said. "She gots a nose for birds."

"She didn't do much when I took her out," Alvin Earl said, flicking his ashes on Granny's azaleas.

"She young. You gots to be patient with her and feed her good."

"What? I told you not to feed her much. Dogs hunt bet-ter when they're real hungry."

"If a dog be hungry, Mr. Alvin Earl, they likely to chew on the birds when they picks 'em up," Little George said. "You wanna watch her work? She do real good without the cord. And she love bein' out in the field. Her point steady as a soldier."

"Not now. I've got business in town. You and Cotton need to finish fixing those fences."

"Yes, suh." Little George motioned to me and handed me Lady's cord. "Lucas can put her up. He real good with her."

Little George and Cotton headed toward the shed and I took Lady to the kennel. Alvin Earl crossed the yard and walked toward the kennel right behind me. I could feel his eyes on me, but I kept my distance.

"If she's as good a dog as Little George says, I'll breed her a couple times a year," he said. "I can sell her pups $85 each."

"She's not a puppy machine." I gave Lady a quick pat on the head as I put her in the kennel.

"What are you talking about?"

"Granny says it's as hard on a dog to have a litter each year as it is on a woman to have a baby."

"What does she know? She never dropped any champions. Look at your mother and that imbecile Robert."

I spun around to face Alvin Earl, furious that he had mentioned my mother. "There was nothing wrong with my mother."

"She got herself killed with your father—didn't she?"

"It was an accident, everyone knows that. A drunk driver went through a red light," I shot back, shaking all over. He had no right to say anything about my parents or the accident.

"They had no business being in Macon in the first place."

"They were going to the hospital for Daddy's X-rays. He was having chest pains—they were afraid he might have a heart attack."

"Your daddy had all kind of problems. He never made any money teaching at that college, and he couldn't get a real job."

"He would have been promoted and gotten a raise if he hadn't been killed," I screamed. "Granny said he probably would have been the head of the history department."

"What does she know?"

"She saw the letter the college dean wrote to my daddy. I've seen it, too."

"Oh, yeah?"

"Yeah," I said, getting control of myself. "And she knows what happened to my money and so do I."

"What the hell are you talking about?"

"I'm talking about the money you took from my drawer back in the spring."

"You think I took your money?" He edged toward me.

"You're the only one except for Granny and Corinthia who's been in our bedroom," I said, determined not to back down.

"If you think that's any proof, you're not nearly as smart as you think you are. That boy probably took it."

"Robert wouldn't take it! He's not a thief. And he doesn't buy liquor."

Laughing in my face, he said, "You think I took your money to buy liquor?"

"You took just enough to buy a bottle of something hard."

"Well, the money's gone and all you got to worry about now is grooming Lady. You hear?" He hurried over to his pickup and got in, revving his engine.

Still fuming, I picked up a big rock. I threw it at the back fender as hard as I could as he tore out of the yard. It glanced off the shiny metal with a sharp ping. I shook my fist in the air and slowly raised my middle finger at him.

Alvin Earl slammed on his brakes and backed up, almost hitting me when he stopped in the drive. His door flew open, and he rushed out to examine his rear fender. "Did you throw that rock?"

"Why would I throw a rock at your truck?" I asked, trying to keep my voice steady. Stuffing my hands in my pockets, I forced myself to walk rather than run away.

"Get back here! I asked you a question and you'd better answer it."

"You must have churned up some gravel when you tore out of the yard." I turned and slowly headed toward the house.

## 29

Alvin Earl was gone for the next few days, but no one was sure where he'd gone. Cotton thought he was visiting some lady friend near Macon. I hoped he'd stay in Macon or wherever, especially after Corinthia told us about a phone call she got while we went to the post office and bank in Crisscross.

"Some man call here while y'all in town, Miz Lettie," said Corinthia as Granny, Robert, and I came into the kitchen. "Y'all want some tea?"

Robert sat down at the table, waiting for his tea. I put the three-cent stamps on the kitchen counter, wondering if Gus or one of the other men from Gordy's had called.

"Did he want to talk to me?" asked Granny, waving a fan from Duncan's Funeral Home in front of her face.

"No, he wanna talk to Mr. Alvin Earl 'bout some business. He say his name Mr. Moretti or somethin' kinda foreign like."

"Moretti—I don't know anyone by that name in Criss-cross." Turning to me, Granny asked, "Lucas, is there a family at school named Moretti?"

"I don't think so." I glanced out the window to see if there was a Buick with a shiny grill and whitewalls cruising by the house. "And I know most of the kids at school."

"He not from 'round here," said Corinthia. "He talk kinda funny—like he from someplace overseas."

"Did he say what he wanted?" asked Granny, patting her neck with her handkerchief.

Corinthia refilled Robert's glass. "No, he just say to have Mr. Alvin Earl call him as soon as he come home today. He say he gots his number."

"Maybe it's someone calling about Lady's papers," Granny said. "Give him the message when he gets back."

"Who know when he get back, Miz Lettie? He never tell me his schedule."

"He can stay away from the farm for good for all I care," I said. "Lady doesn't need any papers to prove she's a good dog. Just ask Little George."

While Alvin Earl was driving around South Georgia looking for a stud, I kept my eye out for the Buick. And I started to feed Lady, giving her a little extra chow each day. Robert and I cleaned out her pen and put in fresh straw. We exercised her in the field next to the house with and without her check cord, and sometimes we threw a couple of old socks rolled into a ball so she could practice retrieving.

"Go get it, girl," I shouted, tossing her the sock ball in the yard.

"Go get it!" echoed Robert.

"She real quick," Little George said, "and she look sharp."

"Cotton told me you used to train dogs for field trials on the big hunting plantations," I said to Little George.

142

"That a long time past. But anybody can train a dog, Lucas, if they be patient."

"Anybody except Alvin Earl," I said. "Lady's scared of him."

"He's mean," said Robert.

Little George pretended he didn't hear our comments. "You don't need no education to be a trainer. And you gonna be goin' off to college in a couple a years."

"I guess. Granny wants me to be a preacher or a lawyer. But I don't want to be shut up in a church or a courtroom all day. I want to do some traveling and see the ocean."

"Once you gets through your schoolin,' you can do lots a things. Nathan T. was gonna be a vet and open up some kinda clinic. He always real good with animals," Little George said, turning from me so I couldn't see the tears in his eyes.

"I remember," I said.

Looking at Lady, he said, "Don't work her too hard, Lucas. You don't wanna wear her out."

"This dog was born to retrieve," I boasted as she dropped the sock at my feet.

"She gots good instincts and she smart, but it real hot today. Let her rest some."

"I'll get her some water and groom her," I said, rubbing her ears.

When I took her back to the kennel and brushed her, I noticed her teats standing up. I wondered if she'd been bred before Alvin Earl brought her to the farm. I talked to Little George when I went by the pump house to get her some fresh water.

"I think Lady's going to have some pups," I said. "Her belly's filling out."

"I thinks you right, Lucas. She sleepin' a lot more than usual. We gots to get her a box and some old towels."

"Do you think she's been bred?"

"Maybe—we gots no way a knowin'. She mighta got with some mut roamin' 'round 'fore Mr. Alvin Earl got her. He ain't got no papers on her and likely never will."

"What's he going to say if she did get with some mutt?"

"I don't know. But it ain't gonna be good."

## 30

During the next two weeks, Alvin Earl spent most of his time playing cards at Gordy's and talking with folks who had bird dogs. Some days he'd come home late at night, and sometimes he'd be gone for several days. Cotton told us he was driving all over Georgia looking for the perfect stud. And I was afraid to think what was going to happen when Lady had her pups.

"Some folks ain't got no sense," said Corinthia as she put away the supper dishes and reached for her fly swatter. "That man could buy three champion dogs for what he payin' out for gas. He think money grow on trees."

"I'm just thankful he's out of the house." Granny sighed, sipping a glass of tea.

"Me, too," said Corinthia. "Things gets ugly when he 'round."

"Y'all better stop being thankful," I said, glancing out the screen door. "I see his truck."

"Yeah, I see his truck," Robert echoed.

"And you know he wanna have somethin' to eat," grumbled Corinthia.

Alvin Earl flung open the screen door and said, "Fix me a sandwich, Corinthia. I ain't had a thing to eat all day."

"I gots the kitchen all cleaned up, but I see what I can find," said Corinthia, going into the pantry.

"Make it snappy," Alvin Earl said. "I found two possible studs—they belong to a farmer down in Peterson County. But I want to see their papers to check their bloodlines."

"Did you ever get the papers for Lady?" I asked.

Ignoring me, he slammed the screen door and went out to the kennel. When he came back to the kitchen, he said, "Y'all are feeding her too much and she needs to get more exercise. She's getting fat—I can't breed a fat bitch."

"Yes, sir," I said, dreading what Alvin Earl would do when he found out she was having pups.

Early the next day he headed out to make some final arrangements with the breeders in Peterson County. After I finished weeding Granny's garden, I went straight to Lady's pen and found her stretched out on the blanket panting. Little George stood close by whispering, "It gonna be all right, little Lady. Your pups comin'."

The next morning we all hurried out to the kennel and saw six tiny puppies nestled next to Lady. They were smaller than a man's fist. Their heads were about the size of a little Christmas ornament, and they made soft whimpering sounds.

"You're taking good care of your pups, girl," I said, watching her nose the pups and lick them.

"She's a good mother," Robert said and reached for a pup.

"Hold on," Little George said, putting his hand out as he stooped down next to the whelping box. "When they gets a little bigger and opens their eyes, y'all can handle 'em and play with 'em. They needs to get use' to bein' 'round folks. But now they gots to stay close to their mother."

"They're real cute, but what's Alvin Earl going to say when he sees them?" Granny asked. "If these pups are mutts, he'll never be able to sell them."

"We don't know who the father is—maybe he's a champion," I said hopefully.

"Maybe—but he coulda been some stray," Little George said. "I think she carryin' those pups when he got her."

When Alvin Earl came home later that day and saw Lady in the whelping box, he ranted and raved like a crazy man. As he got closer to the pen, Lady growled at him, baring her teeth. Cursing loud enough for folks in Crisscross to hear, he grabbed some rocks and threw them at the wire door.

"That worthless bitch! She dropped a litter of pups while I was gone. Get me that shovel. I'm going to kill those puppies."

I rushed over to the kennel door. "Don't hurt them. They're just little puppies."

"Yeah, they're just puppies," echoed Robert.

"They're mutts!"

"How do you know?" Lacing my arms across my chest, I blocked his way. "Are you a vet?"

"Get out of here! I know a hell of a lot more about dogs than you do."

"Then you should know you can't tell much about pups until they're older," I said without moving an inch.

Little George rushed out of the shed, blowing air through his lips in a silent whistle. "What's goin' on, Mr. Alvin Earl?" he asked, as if he didn't know.

"That dog dropped a litter of mutts." Alvin Earl stepped back, wagging his finger at Lady. "The owner tricked me—he just wanted to get rid of her. Instead of giving me cash, he gave me that bitch and told me she had papers."

"Did he give you her papers?" I asked. "Did you ever see them?"

"Hell, no! He didn't give me anything but trouble. And I already got enough trouble with you and that boy." He pointed to Robert as if he were a piece of trash on the side of the road.

"Mr. Alvin Earl, you don't know those pups is mutts," Little George said. "You gots to wait and see."

"Wait and see?" His lip curled and he squinted his eyes. "What do you mean—any fool can tell those pups be mutts."

"They too young. It be easier to see the color when they gets older—you gots to wait 'til they a few weeks old," Little George repeated.

"That's what I told him," I said with a sense of satisfaction.

Alvin Earl stomped off toward his truck and mumbled under his breath just loud enough for us to hear. "Y'all think you know everything. But you don't know nothin'."

### 31

The day after the puppies were born, Granny and I sat on the back porch hoping to catch a breeze while we snapped some beans for supper. "Little George is going to make a quick trip into town tomorrow morning, Lucas," said Granny. "Do you want to go with him?"

"I don't want to leave the puppies," I said. "You never know what Alvin Earl might do."

"He drove off late last night—who knows when he'll be back?" she said. "But even if he does come back, Lady won't let him near those pups."

"Well, okay. I've got some bottles to return." I didn't say anything to Granny, but I also wanted to see Amelia and check on the Cushman scooter at Jenkins' Hardware.

Granny took a sip of her tea. "You'll have to ask Little George if he has time to go by the grocery. I know he's going by the seed and feed store and Gordy's Garage."

"What about Robert?" I popped the end off a bean with my thumbnail.

Granny never let Robert go to Crisscross without her. She was always afraid something would happen to him. She knew that older kids made fun of him and called him "Flat Face" and "No Neck."

"He can stay here with me—this is just a quick trip." Granny put her tea glass on the table and added, "But if you see Mr. Murman, tell him I'll bring some fresh eggs by the grocery next week."

Figuring I wouldn't have to deal with Robert, I went into my room and pulled the scrap of paper with Amelia's telephone number on it out of my drawer. I'd already memorized her number, but I wanted to have the paper just in case. Later that day when the house was quiet and Robert was out in the chicken coop, I called her.

When I heard her say "Hello," I could barely speak. Taking a deep breath, I said, "This is Lucas Webster."

"I thought it might be you." I could tell by her voice that she was glad I'd called. I told her I'd be hanging around the square in the morning and would like to see her.

"If my grandmother doesn't have anything she wants me to do tomorrow, I'll try to come by."

The next day I got up earlier than usual, ready to go to Crisscross without Robert. I wolfed down a piece of sausage and went out to meet Little George on the porch. But when Robert came into the kitchen and saw me with the bottle crates, he knew exactly where I was going.

"Momma, I want to go to town." He shoved some sausage in his mouth and wiped his fingers on his overalls. "I want to go, too."

"Don't talk with your mouth full, Robert," said Granny. "I need you to water my roses this morning."

Shaking his head, he said, "I want to go with Lucas."

Little George stood at the back door and said, "You don't have to worry none, Miz Lettie. We won't be gone long and I watch out for him."

"Let me go, Momma," he pleaded. "I'll be good."

Nodding, Granny turned to Robert and said, "All right, you can go, but you'll have to water the roses after supper. You stay with Lucas, and when Little George tells you it's time to go, you get in the truck."

"Lucas, don't let Robert out of your sight," she said to me.

I frowned. I hated making even a quick trip into town with my uncle tagging along behind me. Even the folks who'd seen him before stole looks and whispered to each other as he shuffled along the sidewalk in his denim overalls. Mothers told their kids not to stare, but the kids would sneak peeks and ask, "What's wrong with that man with the big glasses?" or "Why does that man talk so funny?" Sometimes they even crossed the street to avoid getting too close to him.

Robert never seemed to notice the stares or whispers, but I did. And Granny did, too, though she never said anything.

As we walked toward the truck, Little George said in a low voice, "If folks start sayin' stuff 'bout Robert in town, just 'member they don't know he afflicted. Sometimes they gets scared when they sees somethin' they don't understand."

"Some folks are just ignorant," I said, wondering what Amelia would think of Robert.

"For sure," agreed Little George. "They don't know he wouldn't hurt a flea."

When we got to town, it was already getting hot, and most of the stores were just starting to open. Sheriff Norton's car was parked in the reserved spot, and a few boys from the elementary school were racing around the square on their bikes, stirring up clouds of dust. The usual group of white-haired men was gathered on the barbershop bench with their newspapers. And women were going in and out of Murman's with their baskets. But I didn't see Miss Caroline or Amelia.

Little George eased the truck into a space in front of the grocery, right next to Jenkins' Hardware. I jumped out and ran around to the back of the building. I wanted to see if the Cushman scooter was still in the shed.

"It's still here, Lucas," called Mr. Jenkins from the back door of the store.

Running my hand along the handlebars, I said, "Don't sell it. I'll be back as soon as I get ten more dollars." I cursed Alvin Earl under my breath and kicked a rock across the yard. I knew I'd already have it paid for if he hadn't taken some money out of my drawer.

"Well, if someone else has the money, I'll have to sell it. But so far, no one else has had the cash. And I won't even give credit to the service boys."

I waved to Mr. Jenkins and said, "I'll be back." I went back to the truck, glancing around the square for Amelia.

While Little George went to the seed and feed store, Robert and I returned the bottles to the grocery. Mr. Murman gave me a grand total of forty-eight cents—a penny for each bottle. And I spent fifteen cents on two Co'Colas and a pack of Juicy Fruit. After I promised I'd give Robert a piece of gum later, I stuck the pack in my pocket. Then we looked for a shady spot on the square to drink our sodas and wait for Amelia.

"It's real cold," said Robert, taking a big swig.

"Don't gulp—you'll swallow air and get gas in your stomach," I said, checking the time on the big clock on City Hall.

As soon as he heard the word stomach, he let out a belch that sounded like someone had just fired off one of the cannons on the square.

Wiping my mouth with the back of my hand, I said, "I bet the folks in Alabama heard that—they probably think the Yankees are attacking us."

Proud of himself, Robert asked, "You want to hear me belch again?"

"No, no," I snapped. "I see Amelia heading our way, and I don't want you burping or farting in front of her or doing anything else funny. For once, just try and act normal."

"Amelia—your girlfriend." Giggling, Robert started to chant, "Lucas has a girlfriend, Lucas has a girlfriend."

"Quit and don't do anything funny. Here she comes."

She'd filled out a little since school let out. Even though her boobs weren't nearly as big as Emily Anne's, she no longer looked like a sixth grader. But she was still wearing one of her plaid jumpers.

"Hey, Lucas," she said. "I wasn't sure if you'd still be here."

"We've been waiting for you." I hoped my hair wasn't sticking up and asked, "What have you been doing this summer?"

Studying Robert, she said, "Not much—it's been kind of a boring summer. But I'm going to Atlanta at the end of the month to see my mother and take some art lessons."

"Your mother's in Atlanta?" I tried to muffle a burp.

"My parents got divorced and she didn't want to stay in New York. She's got a little apartment near the Emory campus."

"Maybe we can go fishing one day before you go."

"I want to go fishing," said Robert. "Can I go?" Then he stepped forward and offered his Co'Cola to Amelia. "Do you want some?"

Most folks didn't want to get near Robert, much less touch him. But she smiled and held out her hand. "Oh, no thank you." Taking in the ball of white tape wrapped around his glasses and his stained overalls, she said, "You must be Robert. My grandmother told me about you. I'm Amelia."

Shaking with his left hand, Robert gave her a shy grin and said again, "I want to go fishing."

"Excuse me?" Tilting her head, she tried to figure out what he said.

"He said he wants to go, too," I explained. "But he doesn't fish. He just sits by the pond and watches the turtles."

"Maybe we can all go. But if we do, you'll have to put the worm on my hook. I don't think I can do it." She spoke slowly and her voice lost the clipped edge I'd always heard at school.

"I'll bait your hook and give you an old pair of overalls to wear. You can't go fishing wearing that jumper."

Laughing, she said, "Lucas, your overalls would be way too long for me."

"We'll roll up the legs and you can get your feet wet." I tried to picture how she'd look wearing my overalls. "How long are you going to be in Atlanta?"

"I'm not sure—probably a couple of weeks. My mother says it's a little cooler there than it is here." She patted her forehead with the sleeve of her blouse.

"Any place would be cooler than Crisscross in July and August." I pointed to the big thermometer on the front of the Southern States Bank. "It's already close to ninety degrees. It'll probably be almost a hundred by noon."

Robert peered over his the top of his glasses and suddenly said, "Lady had puppies."

"Is Lady your dog?" asked Amelia. "How many puppies did she have?"

Robert hesitated and looked at me. "How many, Lucas?"

"Six," I said, draining the last of my Co'Cola. "They still have their eyes closed."

"How long have you had Lady?" she asked.

"Just a few months," I said. "She's an English Setter—a bird dog. Alvin Earl won her in a poker game and Little George trained her."

"I know Little George, but who's Alvin Earl?"

"He's Robert's half-brother from Paw Paw's first marriage. He owns the farm now." I started to say something about Alvin Earl not being related to me, but Little George walked up to us and said we needed to go to Gordy's.

"I hope I see you before I go to Atlanta," said Amelia.

"Me, too. Let me know when you want to go fishing and see the puppies."

32

The puppies were four days old and getting fat. But Alvin Earl still hadn't come back to the farm. Cotton said he was likely staying with some lady friend. And I wished he'd stay there forever.

With Alvin Earl gone, the house felt cool and quiet. Little George had driven Granny to the bank, leaving Corinthia to sweep off the back porch and Robert to sweep off the front steps. While they were working, I snuck off to the bathroom, the only place I could get some privacy, to inspect the fuzz growing on my upper lip.

"Lucas, there's a big car out front," Robert called out.

Suddenly alert, a sickening feeling gutted my stomach. "Is it blue?" I yelled back through the bathroom window.

"Yeah, and there's two men," he said. "One of them has a big hat. He looks like a cowboy."

"Get in the house now," I ordered, rushing into the parlor. "Hurry up!"

As Robert hurried into the house, I peeked out the front window. I saw Gus standing by the shiny new Buick. But I didn't recognize the tall, thin man wearing dark glasses and a dark suit sitting on the passenger side. Gus surveyed the yard while the tall man got out and headed toward the front porch.

"I don't think he's here," Gus said, a toothpick dangling from his lip.

"We'll see." The tall man rapped on the front door.

"Who that bangin' on the door?" called Corinthia from the kitchen.

"One of Alvin Earl's friends from town," I said with a shiver.

Robert looked out the window. "He's got big black glasses."

"Nobody 'round here wear black glasses unless they blind." Corinthia came into the parlor and pulled back the curtain.

"He's here to collect his money," I said.

"I knowed he'd be comin' sooner or later." She reached for the fireplace poker and stood by the window.

"Me, too—I've been waiting."

While the tall man stood at the door, Gus peered under the porch. Then he strolled toward the side of the house, studying the shed and barn. The closer he got to the kennel, the more Lady barked.

"There's a dog back there with some pups, but nobody's around," he called. "And I don't see his truck."

The tall man rapped again and said, "Get that sack."

Gus walked toward the Buick and opened the trunk. He pulled out a small paper bag with a string tied around its top.

As Gus headed back toward the house, Robert hurried into our bedroom and came back out with his cap gun. I lifted the shotgun off the rack over the pantry door and grabbed a box of shells.

I loaded the gun faster than a hunter who just spotted a deer and said, "I'm going to the door."

"No, no." Corinthia eyed the gun. "We don't want no trouble."

Wrapping my hand around the barrel, I pushed past her. "That guy with the hat's been out here before. We might need this."

"What you talkin' 'bout?"

The tall man rapped a third time and peered in the front window.

"That short guy's been here before looking for Alvin Earl. I remember him."

"And you didn't tell nobody?" She frowned at me. "Well, we ain't got no money and we don't want no trouble."

"Yeah, we don't want no trouble," echoed Robert, waving his cap gun in the air.

"Robert, don't be messin' with those caps now. Get in the kitchen and stay still," Corinthia said.

I cracked the door open, keeping the shotgun by my side. "This is private property, Mister. Didn't you see the No Trespassing sign? Whatever you're selling, we ain't interested in buying."

"I'm not selling anything," said the tall man said in a calm, deep voice. I could tell he wasn't from Georgia, but I couldn't place his accent. He stuck his foot on the door jam. "My name is Anthony Moretti, and Gus, my associate, is in the yard. We came to see Alvin Earl."

When he said Moretti, I knew he was the man who'd called a few weeks ago and left a message for Alvin Earl. But all I said was, "He's not here. I don't know where he is."

"And you are?"

"I'm no kin to Alvin Earl, but I live on the farm."

"I want to see," whispered Robert, moving closer to the window.

"Get back!" Corinthia hissed. "And stay back."

"We didn't see Alvin Earl's truck. But we wanted to leave him a message and a little gift." He pointed toward the bag in Gus's hand.

"A gift?"

"Yeah, it's a nice little surprise," Gus said, tossing the sack on the wicker table as if he couldn't wait to get rid of it. "You'd better give it to him as soon as he comes in."

"And tell him he needs to call me and set up a meeting time," Mr. Moretti said slowly, emphasizing each word.

"We waited for him today for almost an hour and he never showed up," said Gus. "That's the second time he's stood us up, Sonny."

"I told you before—my name ain't Sonny." I tightened my grip on the barrel.

"My associate didn't mean anything," Mr. Moretti said. "But we'd hate to think that something might have happened to him. It would be terrible if Alvin Earl or anyone else on the farm had some kind of accident."

"An accident—what are you talking about?" I stood perfectly still, waiting for his answer.

"Anything could happen on these country roads, especially late at night when no one's around," Mr. Moretti said.

"If we have to drive out here again, we'll bring a few of our friends. But it won't be a friendly visit." Gus reached in his pocket and flashed his brass knuckles. Then he headed toward the Buick.

"You tell Alvin Earl to open the sack and then give me a call. He has my number." With his eyes on the door, Mr. Moretti backed down the steps. "Remember, Anthony Moretti," he called as he strode across the yard and got in the Buick. Gus cranked up the engine and they tore down the road.

"Are they gone?" Robert asked, still holding his cap gun.

"Yeah, they left in that big fancy car." I stepped out on the porch and stuck the shotgun next to the door. Then, with Robert and Corinthia right behind me, I picked up the paper bag and shook it. It wasn't heavy. But it sounded like something was scraping against some kind of metal or something hard.

"Let's open it," said Robert.

"Oh, no," said Corinthia. "Don't touch it—they left it for Alvin Earl. You don't wants to mess with it."

I gave the bag a final shake. And even though I was curious, I put it down on the table. "You know they'll be coming back. They want their money."

"What you gonna tell Mr. Alvin Earl?" she asked.

"The truth—but he won't want to hear it."

Alvin Earl did show up at the house later that afternoon, and I told him about the visitors. "Mr. Moretti wants you to call him and set up a meeting time. He left you a gift."

"He left me this?" He pointed to the bag and his face got tight. "That man's got no right to come to the farm with Gus. I told him I would work things out."

"How are you going to work things out with men like Mr. Moretti and Gus?" I asked.

I waited to hear what Alvin Earl was going to say. But he ignored my question. He grabbed the bag and untied the string with trembling hands. Then he shook it out on the wicker table.

"Oh, God!" He dropped the bag and backed away. "It's Sam's collar and front paw."

"No—it couldn't be." I stepped closer to get a better look and gagged, sure I was going to vomit. "They cut off his leg—it smells like rotten meat." Caked blood covered the leg that had been chopped off at the joint. A bit of bone stuck out, surrounded by something that looked like shriveled stalks of spring onions.

"That dog was worth at least four hundred dollars—he was the most valuable dog in the county. And they hacked him up like a slab of beef."

"I just hope he was dead before they started hacking him up," I said, covering my mouth.

Alvin Earl's boot shot out and he kicked the table over. "Get all that mess out of here, Lucas. I don't want it anywhere near me."

"What do you want me to do with it?" I asked.

"I don't know. Bury it somewhere. Get that boy to help you." He reached for the shotgun leaning against the door. After checking to make sure it was loaded, he cradled it in the crook of his arm.

"What are you going to do?"

"I told you to clean up that mess. What I do around here is nobody's business. You got that?"

Nodding, I watched him pull open the screen door and step into the parlor. He leaned the gun next to the front door.

"I'm putting it right here just in case those men come back. I want to be ready."

## 33

When I got up on Saturday morning, it was already hot and muggy. And the sun was barely up. I went out on the back porch to cool off. Alvin Earl's truck was parked in the yard and I figured he was still in bed, nursing a hangover.

Little George had gone into town to get some fertilizer, and Cotton was already working on the tractor. I dodged Corinthia and hurried out to the shed before Robert could tag along behind.

Cotton was hunched over the engine. Rings of sweat had soaked through his shirt.

"Hey, Cotton," I said, looking for a shady spot to stand. "You ever gonna get that thing fixed?"

"I ain't sure it worth fixin', but Little George want me to get it runnin'." He jammed a cigarette in his mouth and struck a match on the hood. "I hear y'all had some visitors a few days back."

"Yeah, they drove up in a big Buick looking for Alvin Earl. And they left him a nice little gift." I felt sick just thinking about the bag on the porch.

"They done fixed it so Sam never do any pointin' again, didn't they? Corinthia done tol' me and Little George all 'bout it. I never seed him so mad in my life. He wanna cut off the hands of those mens that cut Sam's paw off."

"Did she tell you I buried the paw out near the barn?" Reaching for his cigarette, I took a long drag to settle my stomach. "I didn't want Granny and Robert to see it."

"No, she just say you gots rid of it." He mopped his face with his cap and said, "Alvin Earl can't keep puttin' Mr. Moretti off—I tol' you that man gots ways of dealin' with folks that don't pay their debts."

"He had some guy named Gus with him, and he had a pair of brass knuckles."

"Gus ain't nothin' to worry 'bout. Mr. Moretti's gots a lot bigger mens than Gus workin' for him and they gots guns."

"Alvin Earl ain't got any money." I took another drag and handed the cigarette back to Cotton. "Everything's still tied up with Mr. Barnett, the lawyer."

"I think Alvin Earl got hisself some lawyer up near Macon, and that lawyer say he can sell parta the farm."

"Sell part of the farm? How do you know that?"

"When I sweepin' up the other day, I hears him askin' 'bout land prices 'round here."

"He can't sell the farm and push us out," I said. "When Mr. Barnett read Paw Paw's will, he said Alvin Earl was supposed to let Granny, Robert, and me live here as long as we wanted."

"I don't know nothin' 'bout wills, but I do knows he gotta get some cash. And he sooner shoot hisself in the foot than put his truck up for sale."

My mind raced. I'd lived on the farm since I was three years old. It was the only home I'd ever known. "If he sells the farm, we'll have to find somewhere else to live."

"Maybe y'all can stay with that cousin Miz Lettie got up in Columbia."

"You mean William?"

"He the man always talkin' 'bout insurance and dress like he goin' to a funeral?"

"That's William. He's got plenty of money and a big house, but he's just like Alvin Earl. He doesn't want to be bothered with Robert."

"Who do? But somebody gots to watch out for him."

"Yeah, that's what I'm afraid of. Granny and I would have to find a little place in Crisscross with a few acres for her garden and some chickens."

"Speaka the devil—here come Robert," Cotton said, snubbing out his cigarette. "He almost as bad 'bout bummin' smokes off me as you."

"He's worse. Don't say anything about Sam and Mr. Moretti. He's afraid of that man."

"Robert not as dumb as folks thinks. I 'fraida Mr. Moretti. And you should be, too."

## 34

The next day it was too hot to eat in the kitchen, so we ate lunch on the back porch. Right after we finished our sandwiches, a new beige coupe pulled into the drive. The grill work sparkled in the sun and the hubcaps had the word MERCURY in the center. I didn't recognize the car, but Granny did.

"Oh, it's Caroline," she said. "And she's got Amelia with her. She looks like she's all dressed up today."

"She always wears plaid dresses and a hair ribbon," I said, hustling out the screen door.

"Robert," Granny said, "we've got company—go wash your face. I hope we've got some of Corinthia's pound cake left."

"Hey, Miss Caroline and Amelia," I said as they got out of the car. "Did y'all come to see the puppies and go fishing? Do I need to get you a pair of my old overalls?"

Amelia giggled. "We won't have time to go fishing, but I do want to see the puppies. And you."

"I'm glad, even if we don't get to the pond," I said, blood rushing to my face.

Miss Caroline gave Granny a hug and said, "I came to see you, Lettie. How are you getting along by yourself?"

"It's been hard for me to get into town since Harold passed," said Granny as Robert came out in the yard. "There's always so much to do on the farm."

"I've been keeping y'all on my prayer list," said Miss Caroline. "I know you miss your daddy, Robert."

"He's with the angels now." Staring at Amelia, Robert said, "I know you. You're Lucas's girlfriend." Then he reached in his pocket and pulled out his lucky penny. "Look what I got."

"Ohhh, how pretty," she said, her eyebrows going up.

She wasn't sure what Robert said and waited for me to interpret. But I shrugged off his comments and said, "Let's go out to the kennel. Just watch your step. Sometimes the chickens get out in the yard."

"They can go look at the puppies, Caroline, and we'll visit on the porch," said Granny. "Alvin Earl's in the house sleeping, and I don't want to wake him."

As we got closer to the kennel, Lady got out of the whelping box and her tail started thumping.

"I see the mother, but where are the puppies?" asked Amelia.

"They're still in the box. They need to be close to their mother."

I opened the kennel door and patted Lady on the head. "Hey, girl. We came to see your pups. Let her sniff you, Amelia, and then you can hold one." I carefully picked up a fat little puppy. "There's four females and two males. This is the biggest male."

"His name is Laddie," said Robert.

"Laddie?" she asked, trying to make sure she understood Robert. "That sounds perfect." She held out her hand to Lady. "Come here, girl."

"Robert wanted to name him Lassie after the dog in the book." Chuckling, I handed Laddie to Amelia. "But then we figured out he was a male."

"Be real careful. Don't squeeze him too tight," Robert said as if he knew everything there was to know about dogs.

"This is the first time I've ever held a tiny puppy." She stroked his head and cuddled him to her chest.

"They just opened their eyes and they're starting to scoot around the box," I said. "If they turn out to be mutts, we'll have to find homes for them."

"Maybe I can take one—I'd love to have a dog," she said. "And my grandmother's got a big yard."

I heard someone walking toward the kennel. Turning around, I saw Alvin Earl, looking like he just rolled out of bed. His eyes were bloodshot and his lips were cracked. And he hadn't shaved in a couple of days.

"Who's this?" he asked with a toothy grin.

"This is Miss Caroline's granddaughter," I said, wishing he was still sleeping off his hangover. "Amelia, this is Alvin Earl, Robert's older brother."

She nodded but barely glanced at Alvin Earl. She was a lot more interested in the puppies than she was in talking to Alvin Earl. And she cooed to Laddie the way folks coo to babies.

"She came to see the puppies," said Robert, rubbing Lady's ears.

"Nice to meet you. I didn't know Miss Caroline had such a pretty granddaughter." His eyes swept across her face and up and down the front of her jumper.

I glared at Alvin Earl, disgusted by the way he was looking at Amelia.

"How long you been in Crisscross?" he asked.

"Only a few months," I said, stepping in front of her.

"I was asking your friend—not you." Alvin Earl pushed
me aside with one hand.

"I know what you were doing," I said.

He leaned toward Amelia and smiled. "You like animals?
We've got lots of animals in the barn."

"My mother always said animal fur made her sneeze."
She buried her face in Laddie's coat. "But it's never bothered
me."

"This heat bothers me—it's a hot one today." Alvin Earl
patted the back of his neck with a dirty handkerchief. And I
noticed the beads of sweat on his forehead and damp rings
under his arms.

"Yeah," said Robert. "It's real hot."

"Lucas, how about you boys get us something cool to
drink," said Alvin Earl, his eyes resting on the front of Amelia's jumper. "I'll take your little friend out to the barn and
show her some of the animals."

"Her name is Amelia," I said, ready to face off against
Alvin Earl. "And she's not interested in going to the barn
with you."

Amelia put Laddie back in the box. Cocking her head to
the side, she looked at Alvin Earl and then looked at me. She
wasn't sure what to do. "Maybe I should just go back on the
porch."

"Lucas is going to bring us some tea out in the barn,"
said Alvin Earl, pushing me toward the house.

"Oh, no. I'm staying with Amelia. You can get yourself
some tea." I'd heard folks talking about what happened to
Betty Jean's younger sister the time she came to visit Betty

164

Jean and Alvin Earl. And I didn't want to leave Amelia any-where close to him.

"What'd you say?" Grabbing my shirt, he dug his finger-nails into my shoulder.

"I said I'll take care of Amelia." I swore silently to myself and wrestled free from his grip. "She's my guest. And I think she'd like to go sit on the porch where it's nice and cool."

"I don't care for any tea." Backing away from Alvin Earl, she reached for my arm. "But I'd like to get out of this heat and sit on the porch."

"You'll have to get your own tea," I said to Alvin Earl. Then I took Amelia's hand, surprised to feel it trembling. And I led her to the house.

## 35

Alvin Earl took off in his truck before Amelia and her grand-mother left the house. No one said anything about what hap-pened at the kennel, but Granny knew something was not right when Amelia and her grandmother left so suddenly. When we sat down for supper that night, she said, "Did you and Alvin Earl argue about something this afternoon? Amelia seemed upset when you came back up to the porch."

"He was going after her," I said.

"Going after Amelia—what do you mean?" she asked.

"Alvin Earl wanted to take her out to the barn to show her the animals." I spat the words out as if I'd swallowed something dirty.

"The leopard don't change his spots," said Corinthia, swatting a fly by the sink. "He never learn."

"I'll try and talk with him." Granny's hand shook as she poured herself more tea.

"That's what you said when Alvin Earl took my money back in the spring." I shoved my plate away so hard the silverware rattled.

"Quit now! Your grandmomma say she gonna talk with Alvin Earl, Lucas," said Corinthia in a loud whisper as she put a bowl of okra on the table.

"Yeah, and even if she does, what's she going to say to him? I've got to get some air." I hurried out of the kitchen, slamming the screen door behind me.

"I'm coming, too," said Robert. "Wait for me."

With Robert on my heels, I crossed the yard to see Lady and check on the puppies. The sun was going down, and Lady dashed back and forth in the kennel when she saw us. The puppies whimpered in their box. As I pulled a biscuit out of my pocket and Robert filled Lady's water dish, I heard Alvin Earl pull up in his truck. He got out and staggered toward the kennel. His face was flushed and he had a cigarette in his hand. And I knew he'd been drinking.

"What's that boy doing here?" He pointed to Robert and flicked his ashes in the grass.

"What does it look like he's doing?" I said under my breath.

"What'd you say?" Alvin Earl demanded, turning toward me.

"He's filling the water bucket," I said slowly.

"Keep him away from me. I want to look at these pups up close. I didn't want to pick them up while your little friend was here." Flipping his cigarette onto the gravel lot, he opened the door to the pen and walked toward the whelping box. When he reached for a pup, Lady growled and bared her teeth. He jerked back his hand in surprise.

"Don't you ever growl at me! I'm the one that pays for your feed."

"She don't like people taking her pups," said Robert.

"What did you say?" he asked, wheeling around to face Robert.

"She don't like people taking her pups," Robert repeated. "And she don't like you."

Shaking his fist in Robert's fact, Alvin Earl stepped toward him. "What did you say? Tell me."

Frightened, Robert backed away. But he tripped on his shoelace, dropping the bucket with a clang. Water splashed all over Alvin Earl's pants and boots.

"Look what you've done. You stupid moron."

"It was an accident," I said through clenched teeth. "He tripped—he didn't mean to do it."

"Quit making excuses for him." Alvin Earl shoved me aside. "Everyone's always making excuses for him."

Grabbing Robert's shirt, he slammed him against the kennel. "And there's no excuse for something like you." He slapped him across the face and then reared back and slapped him again. "Don't you ever spill water on me!"

Robert's glasses flew off, and he covered his head with his arms. He slumped against the wire, tears running down his cheeks and blood spilling from his nose. "Don't hit me. Don't hit me."

"You're going to polish these boots so they look like new." He kicked Robert in the hip. "Do you understand?"

"Stop! Leave him alone." I pulled on his arm. "He didn't do it on purpose."

"Shut up. Mind your own business." Alvin Earl whirled around and punched me in my side. I struggled to get my breath as he pinned me against the kennel door.

I gasped, weaving my fingers into the wire to keep from falling. Ignoring the sharp pain in my gut, I managed to whisper, "It was an accident."

Alvin Earl leaned so close to me that I could smell the tobacco and whiskey on his breath. "If he doesn't stay away from me, I'll really hurt him or you."

Still trying to get my breath, I saw Little George rush out of the barn.

"Y'all gotta problem out here?" he asked. "Mr. Alvin Earl, you'd best calm down."

"Keep that stupid moron away from me." He strode across the yard and got back in his truck. Gunning the engine, he took off down the drive, stirring up clumps of gravel and dust.

"You boys all right?" asked Little George.

Robert sobbed softly and lifted his head, blinking his eyes. Little George helped him stand up. "Where your glasses at?"

"I see them." I took a long breath and bent down to pick them up. "They might be scratched, but they're not broken."

"He hit me." Sniffling, Robert held his nose. "He hit me hard."

Little George handed Robert a bandana from his pocket. "I knows. Go gets a cold rag from Corinthia. That keep your nose from gettin' all swelled up. We be up in a few minutes."

"What about Alvin Earl?" he asked, still sniffling.

"He's probably going to Gordy's," I said, rubbing my side.

"Come on, Lucas. I needs some help in the barn."

While we walked to the barn I said, "Alvin Earl's always had a mean streak. But ever since Paw Paw died, he's been trying to work Robert to death and telling him he's going to kill off all his chickens. And today he beat him up just because he spilled some water on his boots. It ain't right."

Little George pushed his cap up and wiped his forehead with the back of his hand. "Right don't mean much to some folks."

"Robert's his half-brother and he went after him like a crazy man. And this afternoon, he wanted to take Amelia to the barn. Somebody's got to do something."

Little George looked me straight in the eyes. "Lucas, a colored man can't go up against a white man in the South. A colored man can't even get a drink from the same water fountain as a white man, you knows that." He hesitated a minute, shifting his weight to his good leg. "When I 'bout your age, I seed my best friend's daddy danglin' from a tree over in Sutton County. His shirt all bloody and he barefoot."

"Someone hung him? What did he do?"

"He stole a screwdriver and hammer from the hardware store. When the owner foun' out, he got some neighbors together and they went after him. They drag him outa his house in fronta all his kids. Me and William Henry—my friend—hidin' in the bushes. He cryin' and wanna help his daddy. But I held him back—I knows there nothin' he could do."

"Where was the sheriff?"

"Weren't no sheriff. And there weren't no trial."

"No trial—what do you mean?"

"Killin' a colored man ain't the same as killin' a white man. When all the white folks seed my friend's daddy hangin' from a tree, they stood 'round pointin' at his body and laughin' like it be the funniest thing in the worl'. Some mens pass a bottle 'round, and then they start tearin' off little pieces from his pants for some kinda souvenir. Somebody even cuts off twoa his toes." Little George paused and scrubbed his mouth with the back of his hand as if he had something staining his lips.

"What about his body?"

"A couple days later, after everybody left, he still hangin' there, flies buzzin' all over him. He smell real bad. His neck all twisted 'round, and his tongue stickin' outa his mouth like a big black raisin."

"The sheriff never came?" I knew what he was going to say, but something deep inside made me ask.

Little George shook his head. "His body all bloated-like and he real stiff. My daddy and me cut him down and put him in our wagon. We cover him up with a blanket and took him to his family. The preacher say some words and they bury him in the church graveyard."

After a minute or two, I said, "But that was at least thirty years ago. You said you were just a boy."

"Yeah, I just a boy. But even with all the colored servin' in the war, things ain't changed much 'round here, Lucas," he said in a bitter tone I'd never heard before. "Some days, I real glad Nathan T. not 'round to see how things be."

## 36

The sun was barely up when Cotton came to work in the fields the next day. But he'd already heard about what happened to Robert. And I figured if most of the colored folks in Crisscross had heard about it, then most of the white folks had heard about it, too.

"How Robert doin'?" he asked me when I went out to the shed. "He gonna be okay?"

"We thought Alvin Earl broke his nose, but it's just bruised."

Cotton nodded and lit up a Camel. "Corinthia tell me he all black and blue and his face big as a balloon."

"He looks pretty bad. Granny was talking about calling Sheriff Norton."

"For sure—Alvin Earl mean as a snake. One day you gonna come home and fin' Robert dead."

"That's what I'm afraid of, and I think Granny is, too."

Inhaling, he pointed to a crow perched on the burn pile. "Some folks say crows brings bad luck. You superstitious?"

"I never thought much about crows or black cats." He offered me his cigarette, and I took a long drag. "You super-stitious?"

"I don't turn my back on Alvin Earl when we playin' cards. I keeps my rabbit's foot and my ice pick close."

"That's smart. But he hates Robert even more than he hates coloreds. And Robert's his half-brother." I shivered when I thought about what Alvin Earl could do to someone like Robert. Stooping down, I picked up some rocks and rolled them around in my hand like a couple of dice.

"Did Little George tell you what happen up near Macon a few weeks back?" Cotton pulled down the brim of his base-ball cap to cut the sun's glare.

"He told me about seeing his friend's daddy hanging from a tree in Sutton County when he was about my age." I kicked at the dirt floor and stared at the crow. "But I ain't heard anything about Macon."

"Maybe you should ask Alvin Earl. He likely in on it."

"On what?" I pitched a stone at the crow. It landed close to its feet, but the bird didn't move.

"Some white mens kill some colored folk—a man and his wife workin' on a farm up near Macon."

"They killed a woman?"

"Yeah, Corinthia's sister knowed her and she be expec-tin'."

"What did she do?"

"Nothin'. But a white farmer say her husband messin' 'round with his wife, and he went after him with a knife. The colored man grab a stick and try to protect hisself. He a decorated veteran."

"Sounds like he was just trying to defend himself."

"Yeah, that what folks say. But when they goin' home from the fields, some mens drove up and made 'em get outa their truck. They took 'em to a place by a river where it real quiet. They tied 'em up and shot 'em more than twenty times. And then they hung 'em."

"They shot them and hung them?" I shook my head in disbelief. "What about the baby?"

"They try to cut it out, but I thinks that poor baby die when they shot its mama."

"Why did they hang them after they'd already killed them?"

"They want folks to see 'em flappin' 'round fulla bullets." His mouth twitched and he spat on the ground as if the words were poison.

I shuddered and felt sick to my stomach. "What about the men that went after them? What happened to them?"

"Nothin! The government s'pose to be investigatin' and givin' a big reward for information, but they ain't never gonna fin' those mens."

"How do you know?"

"You think anyone gonna talk to investigators? Colored folks know somea those mens in the Klan. Even white folks scared of the Klan. Nobody wanna get beat up or see a cross burnin' in their yard."

I pitched another rock at the crow picking at the burn pile. The bird flapped its wings, but it still didn't leave its spot on the pile.

"Folks real scared the same thing gonna happen 'round here. I scared, too." Pausing for a few seconds, he added,

"You have to tie me down to make me stay here. And if Little George smart, he head North, too."

I thought about the young couple and their baby hanging by the river. "You going to Cleveland?"

"There ain't nothin' here for me but trouble. I gonna try and play some ball. My ol' coaches tell me I good 'nough to walk on. You know Jackie Robinson a Georgia boy and he the rookie of the year. He playin' for the Brooklyn Dodgers now and makin' lots of money."

"What about the cotton? Pickers are hard to get, and Corinthia says the bolls are going to open early this year."

"She the expert." He leaned against a tree and stretched, the cigarette dangling from his lip. "Little George fin' some folks—he always do. He just gots to make sure nonea 'em sticks rocks in their sack 'fore they gets to the gin."

I stared at Cotton and didn't say anything for a minute or two. "Even if he gets the best pickers in the county, it's going to be hard to bring in the crop without you. Real hard. Who's going to keep that old tractor running?"

"I try and tune it up real good 'fore I go. And y'all still got Molly and Jewel."

"Yeah, we still got the mules and a barn full of manure." My voice sounded hard and bitter. "Maybe I should head north, too. I don't want to be stuck in Crisscross for the rest of my life."

"What you gonna do up north?"

"I don't know, but it won't be shoveling manure and working in the fields. Maybe I could get a job with a newspaper."

"You'd be real good workin' at a newspaper, but you gots all your family here."

Cursing to myself, I realized that if I headed north or anywhere else, there'd be no one to take care of Granny and

Robert. They'd be alone on the farm with Alvin Earl. "Yeah, you don't have to remind me. I can't leave Crisscross now. I'm stuck," I said more to myself than to him.

"But your time gonna come."

"Yeah, when I'm about forty or fifty and can barely get around."

"Well, I keeps in touch. I ain't much for writin', but you likely be readin' 'bout me in the sports page. Just in case you don't, takes this so you 'members me." He tossed me his faded blue ball cap from the Crisscross colored high school. "I be gettin' a new one when I makes the team."

I was still pissed with him for wanting to leave. But I put on his old cap and said, "It's going to be real quiet around here without you running your mouth all the time."

Cotton gave me kind of a half-smile. "Yeah, you gotta fin' someone else to get your smokes and you know it ain't gonna be Little George or Corinthia."

"I'll steal some from Alvin Earl."

"Keep away from Alvin Earl and gets yourself onea them ice picks."

### 37

After Cotton talked to me about the hanging and his plans, he sold his truck to Corinthia's brother-in-law. I couldn't believe someone would actually buy that piece of junk, but her brother-in-law paid him in cash. Cotton told me he had enough money to head north and started packing the little clothing he had.

Even though we never went to school together, in some ways I knew I'd miss Cotton more than I missed J.T. I promised I'd look for his name in the sports page and wished him good luck. But I didn't want to go with Little George when he drove him to the bus station in Macon. Part of me was afraid he'd disappear in Cleveland and I'd never see him again. And I think Little George and Corinthia were afraid of the same thing.

A few days after Cotton left, Granny came into the kitchen with a thin white envelope. Corinthia and Robert were out in the chicken coop, and I was finishing up my breakfast when she asked, "Where's Little George this morning, Lucas?"

"He's out in the shed working on the tractor," I said.

"I'm going into town this morning, but I want to give him something from Paw Paw."

"Is it that letter he wrote when he got so sick?" I remembered hearing about a letter Paw Paw had written before he passed.

"Yes. He said I should give it to Little George when the time seemed right. With Cotton leaving and so many colored folks heading north, I think he should have it."

"What do you mean, Granny?" I put on Cotton's old ball cap and wolfed down the rest of my eggs.

"Paw Paw wanted Little George to know he had a place here on the farm." Studying my face carefully, she added, "This letter may affect you, too."

"Me? Why me?"

"This farm may eventually become yours. Paw Paw wanted it to stay in the family."

"I know, Granny, but I'm not sure I'll be staying in Crisscross." I liked working in the fields with Little George. But I didn't want to spend the rest of my life worrying about how much rain we were going to get and trying to bring in a crop every year.

"You've got some time to decide. You can always keep the property and get some tenants to work it. Mr. Barnett will help you. Now let's find Little George."

We walked out to the shed and I thought about letting someone else farm the land. Some people did it, but nobody I knew made much money on tenants working a hundred acres. They had to buy seed and have a place for the tenants to live. And they still had to pay taxes.

Little George was stacking some wood when Granny and I got to the shed. "You needs me, Miz Lettie?" he asked.

"I have a letter I've been meaning to give you," she said. "Mr. Harold wrote it a month or so before he passed."

"I ain't got my glasses. You wants me to try and reads it now?" Little George put down his armload of logs and wiped his hands on his overalls.

"Yes. You might have some questions." She handed him the white envelope with his name written in Paw Paw's sprawling script.

Pulling out his pocketknife, Little George carefully slit open the letter. He sat down on a sawhorse, and after he read it, he looked at my grandmother and slowly read it again. Then he looked at both of us. "Mr. Harold say my daddy and him be half-brothers. That true, Miz Lettie?"

Granny brushed a couple of stray hairs off her forehead and nodded.

"What? I don't understand." I tugged on the brim of Cotton's cap, trying to work out the family connections in my head.

"Paw Paw's daddy was involved with Little George's grandmother," Granny said. "She was just a young girl, but they had a son named George. He was Paw Paw's half-brother and Little George's daddy."

"My momma always tol' me I real light cuz I had some Cherokee blood in me." Little George scratched his head and paused for a minute. "But I guess I be Mr. Harold's half-nephew or somethin' like that."

"I think Granddaddy Watson tried to hide his relationship with your grandmother," said Granny. "She was a lot younger than he was."

"Mr. Harold say his daddy never wanna claim my daddy as his son. And my daddy never say much 'bout his daddy." Little George waved the letter in the air. "I guess our granddaddy 'shamed."

"Maybe your daddy never knew anything about Granddaddy Watson," said Granny.

"I don't know," said Little George. "My daddy not 'round much when I growin' up. My momma pretty much raise us up."

"There's nothing about your daddy in the family Bible," I said, wishing I had a cigarette.

"Back then, nobody wrote down mixed births in the Bible, and I doubt that there's any kind of birth certificate." Granny shook her head and went on. "Somehow Mr. Harold found out about it and tried to make things right. He was always partial to you and wanted you to have part of the farm."

We were all silent for a minute. "So am I kin to Little George?" I asked.

"No, you're not, but Alvin Earl and Robert are, and so is Cotton since his mother was Little George's sister and he's Little George's nephew," said Granny.

Nudging Little George's shoulder, I said, "I always felt like you were family even if we weren't blood kin. You taught me the names of all the plants and trees and how to bait a hook. And I remember riding around on the tractor with you when I was just a little kid."

"Yep, you and Robert loved gettin' on that tractor," he said, standing up and shifting his weight to his good leg. "Y'all could ride for miles."

"But Alvin Earl would never admit to being kin to you or any other colored man. He'd die first," I said.

"I 'spect most white folks feels that way. You know 'bout this, Miz Lettie?" asked Little George, folding and unfolding the letter again.

"Yes, I suspected something long before Mr. Harold told me. He never wanted to talk about his family history, but he always said you weren't the ordinary colored man."

"Mr. Alvin Earl and that lawyer know 'bout this?"

"I think Mr. Barnett knew even before he drew up Mr. Harold's will, and maybe Alvin Earl did, too. He knew his daddy favored you," said Granny.

"I never could figure out why Alvin Earl so hateful all these years." Little George looked at the letter again. "I never ask his daddy for nothin' but a fair wage. Givin' me that land be Mr. Harold's decision."

"And he made it of his own free will," Granny said, smoothing down the collar of her dress. "Now I've got to finish getting ready. Corinthia's driving me into town this morning to pick up some coffee and sugar."

"I'm going to help Little George work on the tractor," I said.

"That tractor need a lot more help than we gots to give," he said. "Cotton s'pose to tune it up 'fore he left. But it still runnin' rough."

"He couldn't wait to get out of here, and Paw Paw was afraid you'd want to go, too."

Squeezing his eyebrows together with his thumb and forefinger, Little George sighed. "Mr. Harold done passed and I gonna be fifty in a few years, Lucas. This letter ain't worth much now—it just a piece a paper with a buncha words on it. It ain't anything official-like."

"You don't think it's going to change things much." My comment was more of a statement than a question, but I waited for his answer.

"Not in Crisscross or anywhere else in Georgia. You think Alvin Earl or most other white folks gonna treat me much different?"

I thought about the decorated veteran and his wife shot and hung near Macon. And I slowly shook my head.

"Even if folks knows I kin to your Paw Paw and got forty acres, they still gonna look at me like a colored man. And they still gonna figure I ain't got much to say." He was quiet for a few seconds and then added, "But you does."

"Not when Alvin Earl's around."

"You a lot smarter than Alvin Earl. And he know it. You gonna fin' a way to deal with him."

## 38

The August heat bore down on the farm like a big heavy hand. We all missed Cotton, and even Little George was short-tempered and out of sorts. The days were filled with burning hot sun. There was no hope of a breeze or rain. And we rubbed kerosene on our faces and hands to ward off the constant swarms of gnats.

No one talked about the letter or mentioned Little George's connection to the family. Alvin Earl disappeared for a while, and Corinthia said he was likely staying with his lady friend in Macon. But one evening after Little George had gone home and Granny and Robert were in the house, he drove up to the yard. As I was putting out fresh water for Lady, he got out of his truck and staggered toward the pen with a gunnysack in his hand.

"You're such a good mother, Lady." I rubbed her head and slipped her a biscuit. "Pretty soon your puppies will be ready for some biscuits, too." They were all crawling around the box and wagging their tails. Laddie, the biggest male, was exploring the pen and making high-pitched barking sounds.

Without saying a word, Alvin Earl opened the gate. His eyes were watery and his shirt was ringed with sweat. He looked at the pups for a minute and then grabbed Laddie. I felt Lady's body get tense and she let out a low growl.

"What are you doing?" I asked.

"None of your business." Cursing, he flipped Laddie upside down, raking his fingers through his coat. Laddie wiggled and squealed. "There's no markings on him or any of the others." He tossed Laddie in his sack like a dirty rag. Then he grabbed two more pups and dropped them in the sack. "These pups ain't purebreds. And I can't sell these mongrels."

I could hear the pups whimpering. "They're going to be good dogs—they've got a smart mother."

"Mutts don't point." As Alvin Earl picked up two more pups and threw them in the sack, Lady bared her teeth and growled again. He kicked her with his boot. "Stay back."

Lady howled and I shouted, "Don't kick her. You'll break her ribs."

"I've wasted enough time and money on these dogs." He snatched up the last pup. "I'm going to throw them in the creek."

"No, stop! Don't drown them. You're just like Mr. Moretti." I tried to grab the sack from him, but he yanked it away from my grasp.

"I'm worse," he said as if he were proud of himself. "These are my pups. I can do whatever I want with them." He pulled a bit of rope out of his pocket and wrapped it around the top of the sack.

"I can find homes for them—there's kids in town that'll take a pup," I said over Lady's short, desperate yelps. When I tried to grab the sack again, he pushed me to the ground. I hit my head on the kennel post and bits of gravel cut into my palms.

"You think that Jew girl wants a pup? You're as crazy as that boy. Nobody wants to feed a worthless mongrel. Just like I don't want to feed you or that boy."

"I got some money saved up, and Robert and I can get jobs," I argued, pushing myself to my feet. "We can pay for their food."

"Who'd hire that idiot? He can't even carry a bucket of water. He should be in the state asylum, and he'd be there now if it weren't for your grandmother."

"Robert's fine right here—he's not hurting you. He's never hurt anyone," I yelled over Lady's frantic barking.

"I'm real tired of your lip." He reared back and slapped me across the face.

My head snapped back. I tasted blood in my mouth. The yard and everything around me was spinning, but I stayed on my feet. Shaking my head to clear my senses, I grabbed the shovel next to the kennel. "Put that sack down before I beat your head in."

"You can't even shoot a bird, you little pussy."

"Set the sack down," I repeated, the muscles in my shoulders and arms tight. Planting myself in front of him, I swung the shovel back like a baseball bat.

Alvin Earl's eyes flashed. "If you're going to kill me with a shovel, at least wipe all the dog shit off of it."

"A little shit shouldn't bother you. It never has before." I tightened my grip, ready to strike. "Set the sack down!"

"Put that shovel down before I break both your arms."

I took a step toward him. "Set that sack down."

"No, Lucas, no," shouted Corinthia, rushing out of the kitchen with the broom. Robert trailed behind with the fireplace poker. Throwing her broom to the ground, she wrapped herself around my arm.

"Where's the puppies?" hollered Robert, waving the poker at Alvin Earl.

"In the sack. He wants to drown them. Grab the sack, Robert. Grab it."

"Leave that sack be, Robert. Stay back," shouted Corinthia. "I knows what he wanna do, Lucas, but he ain't worth killin'."

"Let go of me, Corinthia. Let go." I worked to free my arm, but she had me locked in a vise-like grip, forcing me to drop the shovel. "He's going to drown the puppies. Grab the sack, Robert!"

"I'll get it, Lucas." Robert lunged toward Alvin Earl and reached for the sack.

"Stay back, Robert," ordered Corinthia.

"Get out of here, Alvin Earl," screamed Granny, running out the back door. She picked up Corinthia's broom and pointed it at Alvin Earl's chest.

"What are you doing, old woman?" roared Alvin Earl. "Are you going after me, too?"

"I said get out of here." Granny moved toward Alvin Earl with her broom.

"Get him, Granny," I yelled over Lady's barking. "Get him."

"You better go, Mr. Alvin Earl," said Corinthia. "I can't hold this boy off much longer and Robert gots the poker."

"I'm going." He rushed towards his truck with the squirming sack and threw it into the truck bed. "But I'll be back." Getting in his truck, he gunned the engine and tore down the drive.

I struggled to pull away from Corinthia's grip, but she held me so tight I could barely get a breath. "Let me go. Let me go."

"He ain't worth it, Lucas," said Corinthia, relaxing her hold on me. "He trash—cracker trash."

"Grab Lady, Robert," I yelled. "Grab her."

Robert reached out for Lady's collar, but she was too quick. As darkness fell, she darted by him and raced after the truck, barking and howling.

## 39

We didn't speak of it, but the drowning of the puppies and disappearance of Lady hung over the house like stale air in a musty closet. Everything had a shut-in feel to it. Granny stared at the small pictures of my mother and Paw Paw on the kitchen shelf and then closed her eyes and sighed. She said, "Dogs can grieve and mourn just like people."

Every day for the next week, I kept Lady's water dish full, hoping and praying she'd come home. Robert and I searched for her in the woods and along the creek bed, calling her name. I put some biscuits in my pocket, thinking she might smell them.

"She still might come back," I said to Little George when I walked out to the kennel and put fresh water in her dish one morning. "She's probably getting real hungry."

"I doubts it," he said. "When she couldn't get to her pups, she likely wander off and just kept on lookin' and lookin'. Most dogs like that."

"We haven't found her body."

Little George stared at the road and seemed to forget I was next to him. "Sometimes you never fin' a body or any-thin' else."

I knew he was thinking about Nathan T. but I said, "Lassie came home to her master. She traveled hundreds of miles to get back to him."

"I don't knows 'bout Lassie, Lucas. I ain't read many books, but sometimes grievin' dogs goes off by themselves to die deep in the woods. They just ain't got no spirit left."

"What happens to animals when they die?" I hurt to think of Lady wandering through the woods or dead on the side of the road somewhere. "When Robert's hen died, I told him that chickens go to heaven with the angels."

"And he believe you?"

"Probably." I shrugged. "I just wanted to make him feel better."

"You wants me to say somethin' 'bout angels flappin' 'round in the sky playin' harps?" asked Little George.

"No," I said, suddenly angry. "Don't give me a Sunday school lesson—tell me what you think happens to animals when they die."

Little George leaned on his good leg and looked at me long and hard. "After listenin' to preachers talk 'bout the ev-erlastin' all these years, I hopes we all goes someplace beyond this world."

"Reverend Morris talks a lot more about hell and damna-tion than he does about heaven."

"All preachers be different, and I guess nobody really know for sure."

"If there is a heaven, do you think the heaven for people is the same as the heaven for animals?"

"I thinks all creatures has a place in the kingdom, Lucas." Little George paused. He pushed back the rim of his hat with his hand and stared at the empty whelping box. "In some ways, I kinda like Noah and don't wanna be anywhere in this world or the next where there ain't no animals."

"You don't?"

"Heck no. I likes to think Sam be there with both his paws, runnin' through the woods. There be with lotsa other dogs runnin' 'round, and kids playin' with 'em and givin' 'em biscuits and sausages. Maybe Nathan T. and your mother and daddy be givin' 'em biscuits and sausages, too."

"What about Paw Paw? He didn't go to church and he never liked Reverend Morris."

"Your Paw Paw probably not playin' with the dogs, but wherever heaven be, he likely be there, too, hangin' 'round with his newspaper."

"And what about Mr. Ledbetter, J.T.'s daddy? Some folks say he's going to hell since he jumped off the trestle last fall."

"It ain't for us to judge, Lucas. But I thinks God knows that man not mean-spirited or devilish. He never lie or cheat that I knows of. He never beat on his wife or kids. He just so miserable he couldn't stand livin' no more."

After talking with Little George, I wanted to think of Lady and her pups in a happy, peaceful place. I missed them and felt like there was some kind of narrow band squeezing my heart. A couple of days later, when Granny asked me if I'd like to get a puppy, I shook my head and said, "No dog could ever replace Lady."

"I know she was special, Lucas, but you can't keep on looking for her. You're wearing yourself out. Sometimes you've got to get on with your life and let go of things you love."

"Just forget about them?" I asked in a bitter voice.

"No, no, you never forget about the folks you've loved. I didn't forget about your mother and daddy. Did you?"

I could see tears welling in her eyes, but I shrugged and stared at the fan on the counter. "I didn't forget about them, but I can't remember what they looked like."

"That's why I keep all of their pictures in the parlor and my bedroom," she said in a soft voice.

"I wish I had some pictures of Lady and her pups," I said.

"Well, even if you don't have pictures, you and Robert could make some kind of a memorial to them."

"A memorial?" I asked.

"Some kind of stone or slab like the ones we have in the cemetery for people we love."

I still hurt. But I decided to build a little memorial with Robert. The next day, we walked through the field where Lady liked to run and looked for some stones. We found a big one with little sparkly bits of quartz for Lady and smaller ones for each of her pups. After we cleaned them off, I carved Lady's name on the big flat stone with a nail.

"It's real pretty," said Robert, rubbing a smaller stone on his overalls.

"We'll use that stone for Laddie. We'll stack the stones by the back porch and then we'll always have something to help us remember Lady and the puppies."

Robert gave me a sad little smile and nodded.

## 40

The house was quiet when Alvin Earl pulled into the backyard a few days later. Corinthia and Little George had gone into town on that Saturday afternoon. And Robert and I were out in the shed polishing the rocks for Lady's memorial with an old towel.

When I saw Alvin Earl get out of his truck and stagger toward the porch carrying a crowbar, my anger pushed out all my grief. I was filled with red hot hate. I wanted to scream and cuss and kick in the door of his truck. "Here comes the puppy-killer. We need to get up to the house."

As we ran toward the back steps, I could hear Alvin Earl and Granny arguing in the kitchen. "Hurry, Robert, hurry," I yelled. "He's got a crowbar and Granny's all by herself."

"Did you forget whose farm this is?" Alvin Earl shouted, slurring his words. "The only reason you and that idiot are still here is because Daddy wanted y'all to have someplace to live."

"You're not going to bully me. And if you ever touch your brother or Lucas again, I'll press charges against you," Granny said.

"You'll press charges?" He snorted and laughed.

"Robert's your brother," she said. "I'm not going to let you send him off to the state hospital and gamble away our home."

"I've heard enough out of you, old woman!" He drew back his arm and smacked her across the face.

Granny cried out and collapsed in the corner.

"Leave her alone!" Yanking the screen door open, I burst into the kitchen with Robert right behind me. "Don't touch her."

"You're bleeding, Momma." Robert rushed over to Granny. "Your lip is bleeding."

Alvin Earl lunged toward me with the crowbar, pressing the pointed end into my chest. "Your grandmother's trying to threaten me—you'd better not make the same mistake."

"You drowned the puppies, but you can't slap us around and go after Amelia," I said, fixing my eyes on the crowbar. "I know what you did to Betty Jean's little sister when you were married. And Paw Paw knew, too."

"Going after young girls is a crime," Granny said, struggling to stand. "You can go to prison."

"Yeah, Paw Paw's not around to protect you anymore." I took a step back, glancing around the kitchen for some kind of weapon.

"Get out of here, you little prick. This is my house now." He stomped into the old parlor, and Robert and I followed right behind. As we watched, he swept the metal rod across the top of Granny's piano, knocking all but one of her framed photographs to the floor with a crash.

"Don't break Momma's pictures, Alvin Earl," shouted Robert.

"Are you crazy?" I looked at the splinters of glass on the rug. "Breaking the family pictures is not going to change things."

"Robert's still your flesh and blood," said Granny from the doorway. "Nothing's going to change that."

"I don't claim him and never will." Dropping the crowbar, he snatched up the last picture on the piano and threw it at Granny. The corner of the frame gouged her cheek. She flinched as the glass shattered at her feet.

"Don't hurt Momma," shouted Robert.

"Are you all right, Granny?" I asked, keeping my eyes on Alvin Earl. "Did he hurt you?"

Granny touched her cheek and shook her head. Robert bent down to pick up her picture.

"Get out of here," hollered Alvin Earl. "This is between me and Miss Lettie." He pulled out his pocketknife and started carving something into the side of her piano with the thin blade.

"What are you doing?" I yelled.

"If I put my initials on everything around here, maybe y'all will remember whose farm this is."

"That piano belonged to my grandmother and she left it to me," said Granny.

"It's mine now and so is everything else in this house," he grunted.

Crying out as if Alvin Earl were carving his initials into her side, she reached out to grab his arm. But he flung her against the wall with the back of his hand.

I stretched my arms across the polished wood, knocking the Baptist hymnal to the floor. "Stay away from Granny and her piano."

"Shut your mouth or I'll cut out your tongue." Alvin Earl rushed toward me and wrapped one hand around my neck. He flashed the silver blade under my nose. His fingers tightened, digging into my throat until I almost passed out.

"Let him go. Let him go." Robert pounded Alvin Earl's back with his fists. "You're hurting him."

Alvin Earl relaxed his grip for just a second or two and I wrenched myself free. I kicked him in the shin as hard as I could. Dropping his knife, he backed away and massaged his leg. "You're going to be sorry for that."

I stumbled toward the kitchen, but he clamped a hand on my shoulder and twirled me around. He backed me against the wall and punched me in the stomach. Then he punched me again. My insides exploded. I doubled over and fell to the floor.

He towered over me, kicking me in the ribs. "Get out of my way and stay out of my way."

The blows kept coming. I gasped for a breath and rolled into a ball to protect myself.

"Stop! Stop!" begged Granny. "You're going to kill him."

I tried to crawl away from Alvin Earl's boot, but the sharp pain deep in my gut kept me from going forward. I couldn't move. Out of the corner of my eye, I saw Robert edge toward the front door. He reached for the shotgun—the same gun I'd used when Mr. Moretti came to the house.

"Leave them alone," Robert said, raising the stock to his shoulder.

"Put down the gun, Robert," Granny pleaded. "Put it down."

Fighting to get to my knees and catch a breath, I held out my hand. "Robert, give me that. It's loaded."

"He's hurting you and Momma," he said.

"And I'll hurt you, too, you moron. You never should have been born. I should have drowned you with those pups."

"He didn't mean that." Granny stepped toward Robert and put out her hand.

"Oh, yes I did," hollered Alvin Earl. "You make me sick. You're a disgrace to this family."

"You're the disgrace," I said, clutching my side.

"Get back, Alvin Earl." Robert aimed the gun at Alvin Earl's chest. "Get back."

"He's not worth it, Robert." Panting like an old man, I got to my feet. "Put down the gun."

"You're not going to shoot me," Alvin Earl said softly. "Lucas doesn't have the balls and you don't have the brains. Do you, boy?" Lunging toward Robert, he reached for the gun.

"Get back, Alvin Earl. Get back." Robert tightened his grip on the barrel. And a single shot rang through the house.

Granny let out a scream that seemed to go on forever. There was blood everywhere. Alvin Earl staggered back toward the kitchen. Gasping for a breath, his knees buckled and he pawed at his shirt. His eyes rolled back. He fell on the rug face up, his legs stretched out toward the piano. He groaned once and then he was still.

Everything seemed to stop. And the house was silent.

"Oh, God," I whispered. "You killed him."

## 41

A horrible stillness filled the room. I couldn't take my eyes off the bloody clump of flesh and bone that was once Alvin Earl's chest. The smell of gunpowder hung in the air. The only thing I could hear was the ticking of the mantle clock and my jagged breathing. I wanted to say something, but my mouth wouldn't work. I tasted something metallic and realized I'd bitten my lip.

"What are we going to do with him?" I asked when I finally managed to drag my eyes off his body and find my voice.

"I guess we better call the sheriff," said Granny as if she were talking to someone she'd never met before.

"The sheriff?"

"He'll have to make a report or something," she said.

"A report?" I asked, staring at the shotgun tossed on the rug.

Nodding, Granny slowly picked up her hymnal and ran her fingers across the raised lettering on the cover.

"I didn't mean to hurt him." Robert rocked back and forth, yanking on his ear with one hand and his bloodstained shirt with the other.

"I know—it's all right, Robert." Granny set the hymnal back on the piano and walked toward the telephone.

"I don't want to go to jail," he wailed, his chest heaving.

"Don't cry. You're not going to jail." Then she snatched a blanket off the couch and tossed it over Alvin Earl's body like a shroud. It covered everything except one of his boots.

Robert kept on wailing. And I stared at the boot that had been planted in my ribs a few minutes earlier. It was smooth and shiny except for a slight scuffed spot where Alvin Earl's big toe hit the leather. I wondered if they would bury him in his boots.

"Hush now. You're not going to jail," Granny said again.

"Wait, Granny." I tried to swallow and clear my head. My eyes darted around the room, taking in the bits of glass scattered on the floor and the knife marks on Granny's piano. My body ached. I took a deep breath and forced myself to think. "We don't want them to take Robert to the sheriff's office and ask him lots of questions."

"Sheriff Norton wouldn't put him in jail," said Granny. "I've known him since he was a baby, and he's known Robert since he was a baby."

"Sheriff Norton is my friend." Robert looked up and smiled.

"That doesn't matter," I said. "Alvin Earl's been shot. He's dead. If the sheriff starts to question Robert, this could look real bad for him. They could lock him up somewhere."

Granny got very quiet. "Not the state asylum—they could confine him for the rest of his life. What are we going to do, Lucas?" she whispered, frantically picking up the family pictures and stacking them on the piano.

"Stop, Granny, stop," I said. "You're going to cut yourself."

I remembered what Corinthia told me about patients being stuck in tubs of cold water. And I thought about what Cotton told me about men having their balls cut off and being locked in cages. Then I thought about patients dying under suspicious circumstances and their bodies being dumped in unmarked graves. I'd always been taught to tell the truth, but I knew I couldn't let them send Robert away. And that realization was as sharp as the shattered glass from one of the broken picture frames.

"You call the sheriff and tell him there's been an accident," I said slowly. "There was an argument and Alvin Earl got shot."

"No one meant for anything like this to happen," said Granny.

I looked at Robert for few seconds and then picked up the gun, wiping it on my pants. I clutched the stock and ran my finger along the trigger. "I'll tell the sheriff that Alvin Earl went after you and Robert with the crowbar. I had to stop him."

"What if the sheriff wants to arrest you?" she asked.

"Arrest me? I'll tell him I was just trying to protect you and Robert. He knows Alvin Earl drinks—everybody in Crisscross knows."

"But Alvin Earl is dead. The sheriff could still put you in jail and send you off," said Granny.

"They might send me to reform school for a while, but I don't think they'd put me in prison for the rest of my life," I said.

"I don't know. Alvin Earl's dead." Granny clasped and unclasped her hands. "We need a good lawyer."

Robert broke in. "What about me?"

"Don't say anything," I said. "You don't want to end up in Maysville, do you?"

"No, no," he wailed and clutched my arm. "Don't let them send me away. I want to stay here with you and Momma."

"Then don't say anything," I repeated. "If the sheriff asks you something, tell him Lucas had to shoot Alvin Earl. Look at me and say it."

"Lucas shot Alvin Earl," he said, sniffling.

"Right. I shot Alvin Earl. Now say it again and give me that shirt."

"Lucas shot Alvin Earl," he said, pulling on his buttons.

"What are you going to do with it?" asked Granny. "You'll have to burn it."

"No, that takes too long and it might smell. I'll bury it in the garden." I snatched it out of Robert's hands and quickly blotted the bloody fabric on the front of my shirt.

"Go wash your hands, Robert, and put on another shirt." Grabbing his arm, I pulled him close. "And just remember, you never touched the gun. I shot Alvin Earl."

## 42

After Robert changed, we hurried out to Granny's rose garden. Putting all my weight on the shovel, I dug a hole a good three feet deep. I didn't want the coyotes or any other animal going after that shirt.

I dropped the wad of fabric into the hole and Robert started shoveling dirt back in. "We've got to hustle," I said. "The sun's going to start to go down."

We packed down the soil and covered the area with wood chips, making it look like the rest of Granny's garden. Then we went back into the kitchen and scrubbed our hands with lye soap.

"Make sure you get all your fingernails real clean, Robert," I said, watching the water swirl down the drain. I wondered if we could wash away Alvin Earl's death as easily as we washed the dirt and grit off our hands. And I was afraid to think what might happen if we couldn't.

While we dried our hands, Granny called Sheriff Norton and said that Alvin Earl had been shot. He told her not to touch anything and we went outside to wait in the yard. It was still light, but the air was hot and thick. Within ten minutes, I heard the siren wailing along the county road.

Deputy Kelly and Sheriff Norton pulled in the drive. As they got out of the car, the sheriff adjusted his hat and took a small pad and pen out of his pocket. Then he told Deputy Kelly to take a look around the house.

"What's going on here, Miss Lettie?" Sheriff Norton asked. "Where's Alvin Earl?"

"There's been an accident and he's been shot," she said, sounding like she was out of breath. "I think he's dead."

"Let me go see," he said as he strode toward the house.

We all climbed the front steps. My heart raced and my skin was clammy. My ribs ached where Alvin Earl had kicked me. And I dreaded going back into inside. I didn't want to be anywhere near that covered mound with one boot sticking out. But I took a deep breath and willed myself to stay calm.

Kneeling next to Alvin Earl's body, the sheriff pulled back the blanket and checked for a pulse in his wrist. "He's dead all right," he said, dropping his arm and covering his body. "I'll tell Kelly to call Mr. Duncan and bring the hearse." His eyes rested on the blood on my shirt and then swept around the room. "Where'd all the glass and broken frames come from? What's wrong with your side, Lucas?"

"Alvin Earl went after Granny. He broke all of her family pictures. And he kicked me in the ribs," I said, pressing my hand against my side.

The sheriff scribbled something on his tablet and turned toward Granny. "Why did he break your pictures and kick Lucas, Miss Lettie? Had he been drinking?"

Granny nodded. "A lot. I told him I didn't like the way he'd been slapping Lucas and his brother around and neither would his daddy. He got angrier than I've ever seen him. He hit me across the face and knocked all of my pictures off my piano with a crowbar."

"With that crowbar next to your piano?"

"He had it in the back of the truck," she said.

"Is that how you got the gash?" the sheriff pointed to her face.

"No, he threw a picture at me." Granny touched her cheek and winced.

"What did you do when he threw the picture at her, Lucas?" he asked, scribbling something else on his pad.

My stomach tightened and my mouth was dry. "I told him to leave Granny's stuff alone. But he didn't listen. He wrapped his hands around my throat and tried to choke me."

"Wait a minute," the sheriff said, looking at my neck. "Miss Lettie said he had a crowbar."

Glancing at Granny, I realized I'd goofed up and reached for my neck. Then I said, "Yeah, yeah, he did—he had the crowbar in one hand and grabbed me with his other hand."

"I see the red marks," the sheriff said, leaning toward me. "Tell me what happened next."

"I, ahhh, kicked him in the shin. He dropped the crowbar and started punching me. I dropped to the floor and then he started kicking me."

"What was Robert doing?" Sheriff Norton asked.

196

"He tried to pull him off me, but Alvin Earl shoved him against the wall and smacked him in the face."

"Robert tried to stop him?" he asked, making more notes.

I nodded. "But Alvin Earl picked up the crowbar and went after him with it. I was afraid he was going to smash his skull."

The sheriff turned to Robert. "Did he hit you?"

Robert's head bobbed up and down and he rubbed his cheek the same way Granny had rubbed her cheek earlier.

"He pinned him in the corner and smacked him again. He knocked his glasses off," I said. "I told him to leave him alone, but he just kind of laughed."

The sheriff stopped writing and studied my face. "And then what?"

"Granny started screaming. Alvin Earl let go of Robert and headed toward Granny and me with the crowbar. I reached for the shotgun by the door and told him to stop. But he kept on coming."

"Did he see the gun?"

"Yeah, he saw it." My voice got kind of wobbly and I took a deep breath. "But he said I didn't have the balls to use it and called me a pussy."

"A pussy?" he asked.

"Yeah, but I told him I'd pull the trigger if he took another step." Staring at the mantle clock, I took a couple of quick breaths. A patch of sunlight fell on the clock face, showing the hands at exactly six. I heard the gong chime six times. And then I told the biggest lie of my life. "He took a couple of steps. And I shot him."

"You shot him?" the sheriff repeated.

Avoiding his eyes, I nodded. "I had to."

"The gun was loaded?" He frowned and glanced at Granny. "You keep a loaded gun in the parlor with Robert here?"

"Oh, he knows not to touch it," said Granny quickly.

"He doesn't know anything about guns," I added.

Shooting me a sideways glance, the sheriff asked again, "Why do you keep a loaded gun in your house, Miss Lettie?"

Before Granny could say anything, I said, "Alvin Earl wanted us to be ready. Some men have come by a couple of times looking for him."

"Men from Gordy's?"

Relieved that I could tell the truth, my voice sounded almost normal. "I think Alvin Earl owed them some money."

The sheriff stopped writing for a minute. "How do you know?"

"I found some IOU's in his truck a couple of months ago."

"He lets you drive his truck?"

I snorted. "Nobody drives that truck except him. But I have to wash it and sweep it out every week."

"What about Corinthia and Little George? Were they working today?" he asked, closing his little tablet.

"No," said Granny. "They're visiting Corinthia's sister in town."

"All right," he said. "Miss Lettie, maybe you'd better go put something on that cut. Then y'all need to come to my office."

"Your office?" I asked, trying not to panic. "You've already talked to Granny and me."

"I have a few more questions and I need to get an official statement," he said. "Deputy Kelly can drive you in Mr. Harold's car."

"Before we go, I'd like to call Mr. Barnett, our lawyer," said Granny.

"It never hurts to have a good lawyer," said the sheriff.

### 43

The sheriff's office was in an old brick building across from City Hall. Mr. Barnett was waiting for us outside the front door when Deputy Kelly pulled up in Paw Paw's car. Shaking my hand, Mr. Barnett told me to stay calm as we entered the cool interior. The office area was brightly lit and looked much bigger than it did from the outside.

"The sheriff always has to get an official statement in a situation like this," Mr. Barnett said over the hum of the ceiling fans.

"I guess so," said Granny, nervously twisting the strap on her purse and glancing at Robert. "But I don't know what else there is to tell."

"We told him everything at the house," I said, my stomach churning as I looked at the wanted posters on the bulletin board and wondered if my picture would be added to the display.

Sheriff Norton led us down a narrow hallway to a small room with gray walls and a big table. He sat at the head of the table with a folder and legal pad. We sat in folding chairs on each side of him, with Robert snuggled up close to Granny. Mr. Barnett pulled up a chair next to me, and I was sure he could hear my heart thumping.

Staring at the scratches dug deep into the table, I tried to remember everything I'd told the sheriff earlier. I didn't want to trip myself up. But when he asked why I shot Alvin Earl, I forgot everything I'd planned to say. I simply said I had to protect my family and myself.

He made some notes on his legal pad. Then he turned toward Robert. "I just want to ask you a few questions about the shooting." Pulling up a new page on his pad, he said, "What did you do when Lucas reached for the gun?"

Robert fixed his eyes on me. Tugging on his ear, he rocked from side to side in his chair. My stomach flipped over and I was afraid I was going to throw up. I prayed he wouldn't blurt out anything about what really happened.

Sheriff Norton tapped him on the knee with his pen and asked again, "Robert, what did you do when Lucas reached for the gun? Do you remember?"

Mr. Barnett leaned toward him said in a quiet voice, "It's all right, Robert. No one's going to hurt you. Just answer the sheriff's question."

Looking dazed, Robert shook his head back and forth. "Lucas shot Alvin Earl. He shot him."

"What did you say?" asked the sheriff. "Tell me nice and slow."

I held my breath as Robert shook his head again and mumbled, "Lucas shot Alvin Earl. He shot him." Then he said something about the little red wagon he had when he was a boy, and a snake he saw in the yard. He talked about the pond and the dead puppies and Granny's piano, but everything was all jumbled together. I could make out a few words, but most of it didn't make any sense to me.

The sheriff didn't understand anything he said and neither did Mr. Barnett. But before the sheriff asked him any more questions, I said, "He's confused—everything happened so quickly."

"Sometimes it's hard for him to remember things," added Granny.

Mr. Barnett said, "We all recognize that Robert has some limitations. I don't think he can add much more to your report, sheriff."

"I know Alvin Earl had been drinking, but I still need to get a statement for the file," said the sheriff, flipping through his papers again.

"Lucas is a minor, and you don't have any evidence to show that the shooting was anything other than a justifiable killing in self-defense," said Mr. Barnett. "It seems pretty straightforward to me."

The sheriff put down his pen and closed his folder. Looking at the cut on Granny's cheek and the red marks on my neck, he said, "I think you're right."

"No doubt," said Mr. Barnett, packing up his briefcase and giving me a tiny nod. "Most folks probably would have done the same thing if someone threatened a family member with a crowbar. Let's let these folks go home and get some rest."

"Y'all can leave," said the sheriff. "Just stay close by for the next week or so in case there's any more questions."

"We're not going anywhere." I took a deep breath and headed for the door with Granny and Robert close behind.

## 44

A few days later, we had a quiet graveside ceremony for Alvin Earl. We buried him, along with the truth, in the family cemetery. But no one shed any tears or mourned his loss.

After his service, we never spoke about his death or the sheriff's questioning again. Even though there was lots of talk in town, we remained silent. Granny and I agreed that we would not say a word about the broken pictures or the shooting. We told Robert not to talk about it, and he seemed to understand why he couldn't say anything.

At first, I kept my eye out for Mr. Moretti's shiny new Buick and Gus. Even though I wasn't sure what I would do if Gus and his so-called friends drove out to the farm, I kept the shotgun loaded and my ice pick close by. But after Little George told me all of the big-time gamblers had moved on, I relaxed. I burned Alvin Earl's IOUs and Corinthia cleaned his room. It was almost as if he never existed.

While Little George and Corinthia figured out what happened, they didn't ask for details. But one day when Little George and I were out in the shed, he said, "You was in a hard place, Lucas. But you took carea your own."

Glancing over my shoulder to make sure we were alone, I said, "No one else was around to help. I had to say I shot Alvin Earl—it was the only way to keep Robert safe at home."

"You done what you had to," he said.

For the next few months, Little George and Corinthia continued to work on the farm. I went back to school and had a few classes with Amelia. After Granny sold Alvin Earl's truck, she had enough money for a down payment on a new John Deere tractor. Robert and I helped in the fields. Little George brought in some pickers and we got a good price for the cotton crop.

As the days got shorter, Granny started coughing and developed pneumonia. Dr. Trent wanted her to go to the hospital in Macon, but she didn't want to leave the farm. She said Corinthia was a better nurse than any of those women at the hospital. When Robert asked Corinthia if his momma was going to die, she said, "She gotta take carea that garden. She ain't gonna leave her roses or you." I didn't say anything.

One afternoon when I was sitting with Granny and she was breathing a little easier, she suddenly opened her eyes.

"Lucas," she said softly as she reached for my hand, "I want you to go to college and make something of yourself. Cousin William is the guardian for you and Robert. But you'll still have to look after Robert."

"You know I will, Granny."

"You've protected him before, and you'll likely have to protect him again." She mumbled about things that must have happened when she was a young girl and talked about my mother. Then she started coughing and gurgling when she took a breath.

"You better rest now, Granny," I said. "I'll come back later." I quietly left her room, wondering how I would take care of Robert if I went off to college and he was in Columbia with Cousin William.

Dr. Trent came to see her in the morning and evening, but none of the medicine seemed to help. After a couple of days, Granny stopped talking and slipped into a coma. We called Reverend Morris, and Granny died the next morning while we were standing by her bedside.

"She gone," said Corinthia, smoothing out Granny's nightgown. "She at peace."

"Don't leave me, Momma," cried Robert, tears streaming down his face. He stood by Granny's pillow and howled like a small child.

A strange sound came out of my throat, but I didn't want to cry in front of Robert.

"It's all right, Robert. I'm here," I said, resting my arm on his shoulder. "She's going to heaven to be with Paw Paw and my mother and daddy. And I'm going to take care of you now."

A few days later, Reverend Morris conducted Granny's service, and the church overflowed with people. Even Cousin William and his wife drove down from Columbia. We buried her in the plot next to my parents and Paw Paw. And with the help of Amelia, Robert and I planted geraniums on her grave.

I didn't cry at the funeral. But afterwards, when I watered the red blossoms and entered her name in the family Bible, I couldn't help myself. Staring at the fresh ink on the family record, her death became painfully real. And I knew our lives would be very different now that she was gone.

After the funeral, Corinthia and Little George headed to Cleveland to spend some time with his sister and Cotton. Cousin William packed up some of the family pictures and shipped Granny's piano, the only thing of much value in the house, to his home in Columbia. I wanted to stay in Crisscross with Robert. I told Cousin William I could take care of him after school and on the weekends and find someone to stay with him during the day. Despite everything I could say about why it would be best to keep Robert on the farm with me, Cousin William decided to take me to Columbia to finish high school.

Although Robert wanted to go with me, Cousin William made arrangements to send him to Maysville. I argued and then pleaded, but he said it was best for me to go to a good high school and maybe go on to college. While I didn't want to leave Robert, I hoped I could get the college scholarship Granny always wanted me to get and care for him after I graduated. And I planned to take summer classes so I could get my degree in three years.

Cousin William told Robert he was going to a hospital that had a special school and lots of other people like him. As we made the trip to Maysville with Robert, he clutched his Pooh Bear and asked me over and over why we were going to the hospital. I said he was going to have a chance to make some new friends while I finished school. But he still couldn't understand why we couldn't stay together. So then I told another big lie—I said he wouldn't be at Maysville long.

When we wound our way down the long drive on the hospital grounds, I was surprised to see five or six brick buildings connected by carefully trimmed lawns. They almost looked like pictures of classroom complexes I'd seen on college campuses. I began to think that maybe the stories I'd heard about the state loony bin weren't true. But as we got closer, I noticed bars on all the windows and patients dressed in gray gowns milling around the fenced-in yards behind the buildings. And I dreaded leaving Robert there.

After we parked in the visitor's lot, no one said a word. Robert hung on to his Pooh Bear, and I carried his suitcase into the admissions building lobby. The room was empty, but a small sign on the receptionist's desk said, "Please go to the Director's Office."

While Cousin William went to the office, I glanced around the brightly lit lobby. The walls were bare except for a bulletin board and a Georgia flag hanging by the main entrance. An old couch was stuck in the corner next to a broken wheelchair, and there was a set of double doors marked "Restricted Area—Staff Only" on the far wall. I studied the bulletin board where the meal times and weekly activities were posted. Robert stood by my side, rocking back and forth and tugging on his ear.

"Quit messing with your ear and look at this." I pointed to the schedule. "I think you're going to like it here. They have dances every Saturday."

Robert shook his head. "I don't want to go to dances—I want to go with you."

"You've got to stay here for a while," I said without looking at him. "I can't take care of you now."

The double doors opened and two husky attendants dressed in starched white uniforms came into the lobby. The taller one pulled out a key from the thick ring dangling on his belt and said, "You Robert? You been signed in. We gonna take you to your room."

Robert clutched my arm. "I don't like this place, Lucas. It smells bad."

The shorter attendant said, "You gets use' to the smell. It comin' from the cafeteria. It 'bout time for lunch."

"Don't leave me, Lucas," Robert pleaded, "Don't leave me."

"You're not going to be here very long," I said again, wondering what was behind the double doors. "And I'll come visit and meet your new friends."

"Come on now," said the taller attendant and picked up Robert's suitcase.

"You don't wanna miss your lunch," said the shorter attendant, grabbing his arm. "Tell your friend good-bye."

"I'll come to visit and we'll go back to the farm when I finish school. That's our plan." I gave him a quick hug. "We'll plant a flower garden and get a puppy like Lady."

"You promise?" asked Robert as the attendants half-walked, half-dragged him toward the restricted area.

"Yes, I do. And you know I keep my promises." I waved and hurried to the exit, hoping he wouldn't see my tears as I left the building. While I waited for Cousin William, I prayed Robert would forgive me for leaving him in a strange place that smelled like pee and cooked cabbage.

~

Though I'd never been out of Crisscross for more than a few days, I went to live with Cousin William and his wife in their big white house in Columbia. For the first time in my life, I had my own room with a bathroom, but it didn't matter. I felt as empty as Cousin William's big house. I missed the farm and Little George and Corinthia. And most of all, I missed Amelia and Robert.

Cousin William didn't want to be bothered with Robert, and he was always too busy to make a trip to Maysville. I made a little money doing yard work in the neighborhood. And after I'd been in Columbia a few months, I took a long bus ride one weekend to visit Robert.

He was glad to see me and showed me his room and the cafeteria. He introduced me to a couple of patients, but he didn't look good. He was thin and had a dirty band of gauze wrapped around the mole on his elbow. When I got ready to leave, he clung to my arm and begged me not to go. I promised I'd come back to visit again when I had enough money for a bus ticket. I reminded him of our plan to go back to the farm when I finished school. And I hoped I could keep my promise.

I wrote him letters and sent him a stuffed dog that looked like Lady. I said I hoped his new dog and Pooh Bear would become good friends. A few weeks later I got a short note from one of the hospital supervisors saying that Robert slept with his stuffed dog every night. She also said he was practicing his ABC's so he could send me a letter.

Almost five months had passed when early one morning, Cousin William got a phone call. Even before he said hello, something inside of me knew it was about Robert. The hospital supervisor said he'd had a heart attack and passed away peacefully in his sleep. And I hurt all over when I thought of him dying alone in Maysville.

We brought him home and buried him between Granny and my mother. I wanted to pray at his graveside and say something about the good times we'd shared fishing at the pond and listening to the Saturday night radio. My heart was full, but I choked up. I couldn't find the words to describe the loss of my child-like uncle—the clumsy shadow who had been my burden, my shame, and my loyal companion for most of my life.

For the second time in less than a year, I entered another name in the family Bible. Amelia and I planted geraniums on his grave, and I put a small pile of rocks on his tombstone for the puppies. While I'll always regret that I couldn't care for Robert after Granny died, I realized she'd never have to worry about protecting him again. And thinking of them lying side by side brought me some comfort as I walked back to the old house.

# EPILOGUE

## SPRING 1958

After Robert's death, I graduated from high school and worked my way through the state university in Columbia. I got my degree in English and traveled all over the country writing magazine articles. But I kept in touch with Amelia. And after a few years of my dragging a suitcase around and visiting her when I could, we got married and settled in Atlanta. I work for a magazine publisher and she has a small art gallery.

Little George and Corinthia eventually returned to Crisscross. Over the years, they've kept an eye on the property. With the help of Mr. Barnett, I sold some acreage to pay taxes. A young couple wanted to buy the house. But even though it needs a new roof and lots of repairs, I don't want to sell it or the remaining acres. I want to hold on to the property that's been in the family for four generations and pass it on to our children.

While time has blurred the memories and events, what happened at the farm the year I turned fifteen seemed inevitable. Some folks would say it was wrong to do what I did to protect Robert after the shooting. But not all lies are equal. There's no such thing as the perfect truth or absolute right. And sometimes families have to pull and twist the truth to survive and move forward.

I still grieve for Lady and her pups. And I'll always grieve for the parents I never knew and for Robert and Granny. But the farm is the only real home I have known. I'm tied to the land. The people I care about are there. Little George and Corinthia live close by, and Cotton visits them once in a while.

One day, I'll fix up the house and plant a garden with lots of vegetables and old-fashioned roses. I'll cut back the weeds in the family cemetery and scrub the tombstones. Amelia and I will raise our family there, and if we have a son, we'll name him Robert.

# ACKNOWLEDGEMENTS

Writing can be hard, lonely work—but it is much easier with the support of family, friends, and writing groups. Special thanks go to the many people and groups involved in completing *Crooked Truth*.

To neighbors and friends Zeke Carter, Rick Casey, and Jody Lewis, who answered my many questions about daily life in small rural communities and bird hunting. To Gene Ledbetter, a talented graphic designer who provided ideas and sketches for my cover art.

To several lawyers—G. Roger Land, Fred Overby, and Maria Drinkard—who gave me legal advice on preparing wills and trusts. To veterinarians Dr. Annemiek Kuik, who shared her expertise on dog anatomy and injuries, and Dr. Dave Griswold and Kelly Griswold for sharing their expertise on large farm animals and dog raising.

To Lt. Andrea Knight from the Jefferson County Sheriff's Office in Alabama for information on the design and firing of shotguns.

To those in my writing groups—the Middle Grade Mojo, particularly Debbie D'Aurelio and Zona Rosa—for their ongoing suggestions and feedback on the development of my character, plot, and setting. For the interest and support of members of the Atlanta Writers, particularly George Weinstein, who read my first chapters several times and gave me marketing tips.

To Angela Rydell, my longtime writing coach and teacher, who helped me develop my characters and story line as well as my craft. She recognized the strengths and weaknesses in my early manuscript and encouraged me to revise and tighten.

To my many readers for going through chapter revisions and providing thoughtful feedback—Patricia Bowen, Anne Bucey, Susan Carter, Judy R. Dodd, Robin Hickey, and Adrienne Williams. I especially appreciate the close attention Anne and Robin paid to dialogue and plot developments.

To the Mercer Press editors and staff for their many insightful suggestions on my manuscript and their attention to details as well as their guidance in the publishing process.

And lastly, to my family—John Barge, a cousin by marriage who answered my many questions about growing up in South Georgia and raising bird dogs in the 1940s; my brother John P. Anderson, who read many of my early drafts and shared details about his hunting experiences; and my daughter Kristi V. Deprin and my son H. Andrew Webb, who served as both sounding boards and readers.

Above all, to my husband Hulan S. Webb, my oldest, most loyal fan. He not only served as a master proofreader and computer guide late into the night but also accompanied me on many trips around the Southeast to check local records and historical details.

My thanks to one and all.

# Discussion Questions for *Crooked Truth*

1. *Crooked Truth* takes place in the late 1940s in a rural area of South Georgia. How would the story and characters have changed if it had been set in a different local or more contemporary time period?

2. Lucas goes to live on his grandparents' farm after his parents are killed. Who becomes a father figure to him and how does this figure impact his development?

3. Why is Alvin Earl so cruel and heartless? Would he treat animals and other characters in the book differently if he'd grown up on the farm with PawPaw? Do you ever feel sympathetic toward him?

4. At first Lucas and Cotton seem to be very different, but as the story progresses many of their differences disappear. In what ways do they become alike?

5. Several characters warn Lucas about going up against Alvin Earl. What compels Lucas to continue to challenge Alvin Earl?

6. How might the development of Alvin Earl and Little George have changed if Paw Paw had acknowledged the family tie while they were still boys?

7. Lucas feels that Amelia is different from other girls in Crisscross. Why does he find those differences appealing?

8. Several characters die from natural and unnatural causes throughout the book. Who, if anyone, should be held accountable for those deaths?

9. The effects of several types of prejudice are explored throughout the book. What kind of connections can you make between the racial prejudice of the late 1940's and current racial prejudice?

10. Many people in Crisscross look at Robert as the local freak. How has the treatment of people with mental issues and developmental problems changed since the late 1940s?

11. How might the final chapters of the book have unfolded if the local sheriff had pursued the truth? Do you think he knew who was responsible for the shooting?

12. We all tell lies—some little, some big, some harmless, others life-changing. Have you ever felt a need to stretch the truth to hide a secret or protect someone in your family?

13. After reading the book, can you think of another title that would be appropriate for *Crooked Truth?*